PRAISE

"*Heart and Salt* is a satisfyingly beautiful collection of short vignettes. With its glimpses into the lives of a divorcee, grieving daughter, a teen wrought with angst and more, there are few feminine feelings left unmined. These stories are a must for those wishing to reflect while also being transported."
Suzanne Crain Miller, author of *Queen*

"*Heart and Salt* is an honest account of girlhood growing into womanhood, the femininity of each reaching out its hand for the other as if to say, We will get through this together."
Chimen Kouri, author of *Peach Milk*

ABOUT THE AUTHOR

If you see a woman in Doc Martens drooling over a 1964 Chevy Impala like it's candy, it's probably Elaina. Her first two books are *Italian Bones in the Snow* and *Black Licorice*. Elaina's poems and prose have been published in many lit mags and journals. She's the editor of *50 Give or Take* with Vine Leaves Press and lives on the Jersey Shore with her husband and daughters. Her essay "I Said it Out Loud" was a 2021 finalist in the Anne Dillard CNF contest. Elaina is also an acquisitions reader for Pearson Education.

www.elainawrites.com

Elaina Battista-Parsons

Heart and Salt

Print Edition
ISBN: 978-3-98832-002-5
Published by Vine Leaves Press 2023

Cover design by Jessica Bell
Interior design by Amie McCracken

You can be it all, girls.

FEATHER IN THE MIDDLE

First published in Malarkey Books: first chapters

Feather Sierra was rich in middle-ness the way some people were rich in love or friendships. Middle-ness: a state of always feeling somewhere else, not right here or there, simply situated in the middle, even when you're in the heart of life with people who love you. Sort of like a modest little town on the outskirts of a city. Minus the feeling of belonging. Okay, so more like the hidden run-down gas station rather than the town. That gas station with the oil-stained gravel and beer bottle caps as stones. How it came about, Feather didn't know, but to never feel like she was devoted to one space or one person was getting old. And it's not that she couldn't commit to a boyfriend or a friend. It was more a false reality in her soul. You'd never really spot it as an onlooker. It mimicked somatic anxiety, and that's often invisible. You can't see a racing pulse. Don't confuse it with ambiguity because that would imply mixed feelings. She felt things with conviction. It was more about the lack of belonging.

Feather's senior prom was no exception. She was half and half, smack dab in liminal space where her teenage brain liked to camp out—excited for the visuals of the evenings, bored over the shitty color patterns and teased bangs. She wished she had met

Tim a few months earlier so he could've been her date, but at the same time, it would be the last hurrah for her and Eddie. The last time to smell his skin near her face, feel the sear of his heartache, and maybe to say she was sorry once more in his ear during a slow dance. His eternal sub-sandwich breath to her garlic-over-linguini breath. She teetered back and forth in her head about hooking up with Eddie after prom since Tim never said they were exclusive yet. I mean, would Eddie even want to kiss her knowing she was dating the former baseball star from Cedar South High? Eddie was a scholarship track runner, so he had a lot to say about other athletes. He'd say baseball didn't require what track required of him—the endurance and the spiritual connection to something higher than himself.

"Baseball players are assholes, Feather."

They dated for the first twenty-three months of high school. When they were dating, she felt elsewhere most of the time, and he was in denial about it because she was certain he knew. If he could connect to running on an elevated level, then for sure he sensed her distance. Her indecision about who, what, and where would be the death of her, she figured. Either that or Eddie with a pocketknife to her throat while she was asleep.

Prom night was nothing out of the ordinary, especially after months of decision-making with the committee around her. She chose the prom song, rigging it once and for all. Feather could not have a 1970s love ballad as her senior-year song. As senior class president, she earned that much. Yet part of her felt guilty about abusing her power—fixing it so that they had a song of their times, unable to dance to, but instead sway as a group. Way more original to have The Cranberries' "Dreams" instead of "We've Got Tonight." Snooze. She couldn't allow it.

After prom, they all hopped in the cars they were supposed to hop into and headed down to Brickwood Beach, a solid hour from Cedar. Brickwood wasn't as clean of a coastline as Cedar: crushed beer cans dotted the boards, less beach cottage, more junk store. Cedar wasn't pure *family-friendly,* but still closer to it than the messier guts of Brickwood.

"Give me two minutes," she told Eddie as she raced to find her best friend Kelsey and her boyfriend of a few months, Dan.

Dan had graduated Cedar North last year, so he was happy to follow Kelsey wherever. And Kelsey didn't want the Brickwood scene like the rest of the group wanted it—popular kids, a few athletes, and two band geeks—Feather and Eddie. Eddie being the star athlete and first chair saxophone, and Feather, out of shape, former field hockey forward and second-best trumpet player.

"Kels, are you good? Can I go?" Feather asked and ruffled Kelsey's hair that hung perfectly straight down her open back. Kelsey's hair spread across her thin, tan shoulders against her cream gown. Feather's dress was that of a 1920s flapper, unlike the poofed shoulders and giant bows across torsos. Feather's mom knew how to find a dress that spoke more New York City than the reality of their beach-town spandex energy.

"Yes. Enjoy yourself. Use a condom," Kelsey said and tossed her hair with her French manicure. "And be nice to him."

"I'm not sleeping with Eddie. Especially in Brickwood. It smells like hot pee and beer near those hotels. Besides, we still have school two days next week," Feather said and smacked her smooth-as-a-baby-butt arms. Ooh! Feather remembered she had that, too, now. She ripped her arm hair from the roots only weeks ago using a cream from the CVS. "I can't do it then face his droopy dog eyes all week."

"Okay. Whatever. Have fun," she said, and they parted. Eddie pulled away in his Honda Civic before Feather could shut the door.

"Hey. Chill out," she said. "Where's the fire?"

"You're not my girlfriend anymore. I don't owe you manners," he said and accelerated. "You belong to that South Cedar baseball dropout now right?"

There it was. "Oh my God, if this is how this hour ride is gonna go," Feather said.

"Relax. I have the Chili Peppers. We're good."

"He's not a dropout."

"Fine. Not a dropout." He adjusted the rearview mirror and bit his bottom lip.

Eddie pressed play, and the first song was bass-heavy and fast-paced, true Red Hot Chili Pepper-style, all Californian.

"Turn it up," Feather said as she climbed into the tight backseat and changed out of her dress and into a pair of jean shorts and a tee. She watched him try to catch it all from the rearview. "Turn your head. Don't tell me you've seen it already."

As she contorted and slid out of her dress she realized that their years together began with a Red Hot album called *Blood Sugar Sex Magik,* and was now concluding with *Blood Sugar Sex Magik,* their special track being "Apache Rose Peacock." Eddie would certainly skip that track today. They'd done everything but sex, but still. The penetration didn't happen, and from what she'd heard from Kelsey and half the other girls she knew, nothing was close to its effect on a girl's heart and well…you know. Fingers were great and had purpose, but still. Not the same. Kelsey said it was a certain kind of pulsation that you can't shake. She said it was a worthy combination of pain and pleasure that only a tidal wave can emulate.

"But let's talk," Eddie said, interrupting Feather's private pseudo-sex analysis. She didn't want to do anything of the talking sort because she knew his wheels were turning a mile a minute. "Do you love Timmy boy? You do, don't you? You totally want to marry him already, don't you?"

"Are you serious?" Feather zipped up her jeans and threw on some flip flops.

"Are you serious is the question, Feath." Eddie turned the volume dial to the left.

She climbed up front and turned the volume to the right and watched him grind his teeth for most of their drizzly ride up the parkway.

Finally, after he decided they'd breathed enough, he turned the volume back down. "So. Did you formulate your final answer? Me or him?"

"For now, him. Especially the way you're acting. Jesus, Eddie."

"You know we will be the only ones not drinking once we get there. Even Santos will have a beer or two," he said and pulled off the exit for Brickwood Beach. Santos was Eddie's best friend since elementary school, and Feather adored him. The best friend of a boyfriend and his girlfriend anyone could ever want. Kind, loyal, and no bullshit, ever. In fact, Feather was more excited to see Santos than to see how Eddie's mood would roll and spiral and zigzag all over the map of their night after senior prom.

"It's not like he's the first guy I dated since we broke up. Why is Tim bugging you so much? Because you don't ever see us together? Like, literally, see us with your eyes?"

"Yes. If you must know. It freaks me out that you're so into him and I don't know anything about him. You're gonna have sex with him, aren't you?" Eddie sped up through the bar-heavy Brickwood streets and gripped the wheel tighter.

"Well, not tonight I'm not and—" Before Feather could continue the argument, Santos banged on Eddie's back bumper, then hopped on his roof like the agile soccer player everyone knew him to be.

"STOP fighting, you two. I know you are! Get the fuck out here and join the human race," he said, clearly a few beers in. Santos looked exactly the way everyone expected him to look: Adidas sneakers and baggy, red Umbro shorts. "Get out and have some fun, you guys. I'm not breaking you two up for fighting tonight, just to give you fair warning." He motioned like he was kicking a ball into the net "I'm not doing your bullshit tonight."

Feather and Eddie exited the car with their backpacks full of socks and underwear and scowled at each other, hugged Santos one at a time, and followed him into the hotel room already overflowing with classmates. Since Feather changed in the car, Eddie was the first one to find a spot in a crowded hotel room to wiggle out of his tux pants and into the same shorts as Santos, but blue.

Eddie scurried in the opposite direction while Feather found Louis Magenta and his delicious blue eyes meditating like the hippie he was—sitting on a green boardwalk bench overlooking the ocean while his friends smoked God knows what in their vicinity. His guitar friend sat on the boards playing "Black" over and over with a cigarette hanging out of her mouth and a red Solo cup next to her legs. Feather barely said ten words to Louis all through high school, but they'd wave and smile because, after all, he and Feather were partners in second grade during the big fruit-bowl art project. They also had friends in common in Cranford, so there was that meaningless bond too.

"Feather, you looked slamming tonight. Eddie must be dying over there. Look at him. He needs to get a grip. Get laid or something," Louis said, opening his eyes as soon as Feather sat next to him.

"Ha! Yeah, that's not gonna happen. What were you doing just now? Praying over something?" Feather asked. She cleared her hair from her face with a scrunchie and a ponytail, the way Eddie loved it. She felt him watching. She was so cruel sometimes when she wasn't lingering in the middle of an emotion. Knowing he was watching them made Feather edge a few inches closer to Louis. Brutal.

"Something like praying I guess. Hard to explain," Louis said and laughed as he rearranged his crossed legs. I could feel his "girlfriend" Luna's eyes digging deep into her cheeks. And Eddie's weren't far behind. His pants were baggy and had several elephant graphics in grays and yellows. They were held up with a white rope.

"I love your pants, by the way. I need a pair like that." She flirted in neutral. Never in drive.

"Well, first you have to smoke some weed, then you qualify for a pair. Luna makes them," he said. They laughed, and mid-laugh, Feather drizzled her fingernails over his arm hair. Eddie's pulse was surely out of control. Louis barely flinched from her touch.

She stared into his drippy blue eyes and waited for him to laugh and say psyche. Instead, he bumped his shoulder on hers and asked, "Earth to Feather?" He smelled like cherries and weed.

"I'm here. Whatever, okay. I have to get back to..." The truth was Eddie was zero fun and Santos was concentrating on Denise White's boobs. Feather had nowhere to be. Then she missed Tim. Pushing...pushing...herself more to the middle where forgotten things live. Sometimes she lived a few days in the past, sometimes a few days in the future, so that her timeframe was middle-ish too. One minute her eyes were falling into Louis's and the next, staring beyond his face into the horizon.

"Stay with me on this bench, Feather, class prez. We should hang out this summer," Louis said. His hair was knotty but clean, the color of the sand below them.

"Yeah. You think Luna would be okay with that?" she asked, pointing in her direction with the fingers holding up her chin.

"Oh you should talk. I heard about you and the Cedar South hottie. Former starting pitcher." He pulled a fresh joint out of his front shirt pocket and twirled it in his hand.

"Oh my God. Does everyone know about Tim?" she asked and stood up, flattening her jean shorts and tee, noticing her extra curves from quitting field hockey this year.

"Pretty much, beautiful. Listen, go find Eddie and be nice to him tonight. Or you'll regret it forever." At that he kissed Feather's arm and sent her off. Luna's knifey eyeballs were getting closer and sharper, so Feather gave her a fake smile and jogged off to find Eddie alone in the sand. She stopped a good quarter mile in front of him to watch him drink his Snapple in deep thought, tossing random pebbles across the sand until he finally spotted her approaching.

"Come sit," he said, patting the sand like this was a rom-com.

"I'm good. I don't want to fight with you anymore," she said. She approached him as if he were a bear and she was the hiker, not realizing why she would approach any bear. "Let's be social, Ed, come on." Her stride remained fragile, even though with bears you're supposed to cause a ruckus.

"You be social, I'll be dark," he said. "Sit."

"Suit yourself," she said, and unlike any other time in her high school life, she walked away from his mood instead of through it. She walked away toward Louis, his hippies, Alaina Martin and her drunk posse singing "Alive" on the boards as the rickshaw missed their toes by millimeters at every turn. Feather joined them singing for a hot minute, which was met by sweaty hugs in all directions, and then trudged back to the crowded hotel room where they dropped their bags. Why didn't she stay? Every time there was a movement to a side and out of the middle, she retreated. As if it would suffocate her, forcing her to remain present.

Fully hydrated and without an ounce of alcohol in her system, she passed out next to a very drunk Santos in a queen-sized bed that smelled like feet and piss. He was in a tight sleep, so Feather knew he'd never suspect a bed buddy. She also knew he'd never try anything once he did find her when he got up to pee or vomit.

The next morning, knowing for certain he found Feather next to Santos, Eddie sped them home in silence. It wasn't about Santos though. It was about Tim. Everything leading up to Tim, and what lay ahead. Separation with unrequited things. All over the place, on both their parts. Feather in the middle and Eddie on Feather. What they had months ago was pure and real, but then slowly became beyond what Feather could handle at sixteen. He would've eloped if she said the words. She'd never say the words. And now she loved Tim. Yet, in the last stretch of parkway closer to Cedar, she got an ache of being so alone. Like Luna was with Louis. In it. All of it. Eddie is with her. But where was Feather? Tim felt distant even when next to her, but she loved the hell out of him anyway. Or did she secretly love the hell out of the middle?

Before she could sort it, they pulled into her driveway. The morning was overcast. Feather had met Eddie on a day that was just as gray, almost four years ago in August 1991.

It was two weeks before our freshmen year officially began, but marching band was in full effect since they had an intricate field show to train for. Eddie roared in from the junior high on the opposite side of town, along with Santos and many others Feather would grow to know and love. Santos wasn't a musician, but he'd always "drop" Eddie off to rehearsals after a long, hard soccer practice on the fields behind the school. Feather would also be soaked to the bone in sweat from field hockey workouts. Feather swore Eddie liked Liza in the percussion section, all prim and lanky. Feather was athletic like Eddie, but also first trumpet determined to prove her worth to their very sexist band director. Eddie's saxophone lips chose Feather. Soon came the "ask out" portion of rehearsal, in between water breaks and opening counts of "Call Me" by Blondie. Two weeks later, Feather was Eddie's magnolia tree to his oak. Like trees, they spoke an easy, almost cosmic language as a pair. Until they set each other on fire with their arguments. Arguments in the stairwells in between classes. Arguments in the instrument room after practice. Usually, it was over Feather supposedly staring too long at Dan Smith on the soccer team or Mike Prattman in the tuba section.

Every Saturday, instead of parties with the rest of Cedar North, they'd sit in Feather's room and listen to *Blood Sugar Sex Magik* while they sketched or made out. Sometimes they'd meet friends at the movies or the basketball courts, but mostly it was enough to be the two of them. That first year drowned in "I love you" and "Never leave me."

"Give your baseball player a kiss for me," Eddie said, still gripping the steering wheel. Without a wave or a final glance, he drove off. Feather felt nothing because that's what the middle feels like on a good day.

FEBRUARY AND MARIA

February

I believe I'll never be happy again. My belief is rooted in the following: Every book I read says you need to love people and they love you to be happy. Every song is about it, for fuck's sake. If those are the requirements, then I'm screwed. I love my mother and my best friend Dax, but other than them, the shop is closed. I blame my father. As extra, textbook, and standard as that sounds, it's the goddamned truth. He left, it hurt like hell, and therefore my stance to not love nor be loved is my final stance. I yearned for his love and affection for so long, and then got pummeled. I swear I'd never be that wide open ever again. Impervious. My mom and I decided to move, trading sand for soil and fresh crabs for fresh vegetables. We exchanged boat life for sunshine in a big backyard in a country town. We left people for weeds. You get the goddamn gist.

Dax moved to Buffalo, NY for college, so Mom and I ditching our beach town made no difference to me. I plan to enroll in a community college eventually, pick some random, no-brainer career, and be there for my mom for the rest of my life. I'm smart enough for Rutgers, but way too lazy. My mom and I grieved our new life for an entire year as soon as Dad officially moved to Austin with his new family. One evening she popped her head in my bedroom and boomed, "Feb. Enough crying. We're done. Pack your stuff. We're moving to the country." She found a job managing a thrift store, and so that's how I will spend my summer. Slapping price tags on typewriters, old Lenox, and naturally distressed desks. Maybe I'll try my hand at gardening too. I've been known to have a delicate touch despite my overgrown armpit hair and my coffee-stained jeans. We're five minutes from our new house in Lampton, New Jersey, ten minutes from its downtown, and thirty minutes from the highest point in the state. Two hours from the beach. Being so close to an actual walkable downtown feels sort of like a fairytale to me. I grew up with sand between every crevice, and the sun a familiar friend in my face, bouncing rays off the top of the ocean. Mom thinks we're beached out, and it's time for outdoors in a new way. I guess I know what she means, but I will miss the non-judgmental toss of the ocean foam when things feel extra hopeless.

Maria

Dr. Emma wrote that it's smart to open a new chapter once you've been betrayed by the one who was supposed to love you most. My sister lent me Dr. Emma's memoir, *Fresh Canvas.* After Bob split, my heart split into segments like a grapefruit that rich people eat late morning with a cup of Colombian coffee. Bob and I fought all the time for ten years out of twenty. We hadn't touched each other's hands for years, and I gave up on his body next to mine years prior to that. His pillowcase ran cold and rose to fluffy. My heart in segments. February ruined at age eighteen. We're five minutes from Bellethorn Place, Lampton, NJ. Five minutes away from our new chapter—our first home as mother and daughter. Our first home near pine trees and deer. We will have grass instead of stones and broken shells as a lawn. My feet will love it, at least. Feb has a permanent forehead worry line and her shoulders slump, like her eyes. I worry, but my therapist says, "Let her process. And trust that process." Which is a good thing because my soul is bone-dry, and I don't have anything to offer her right now except my presence. Dr. Emma will tell me what to do.

February

1481 Bellethorn Place is the color of November: burnt orange and faded with white shutters feel like a million years old. Some on the verge of breaking off, literally hanging by a particle of vinyl. I get it. I give it one swift snowfall to do the job. We're only renting, so it's fine. It's home now. I grab my navy backpack from the backseat. It's bursting in the shape of magazines. Every copy of *Car Craft* that I own. The only friendship I will allow are these damn magazines. Dax is hours away. They promised they'd visit over Thanksgiving, and even though it's only July, I can't wait. They're my true friend. The friend who tells me when I'm acting like a jerk, eating too many edibles, and forgetting to smile at the local soap makers at the farmers' market when they smile first.

I twist my ratty brown hair in a bun, plop my bag on the uneven porch, and shield my eyes from the noon sun. An old walnut tree stares us down, and we stare at each other. Mom, the tree, and me. I exhale and approach the tangerine front door.

Maria

The swing on the porch needs new chains. Broken bones from a broken swing is not in my budget. Feb's scowl has tilted ever so slightly upward. A few millimeters in the right direction. We're in more of an ambivalent zone now, which I'll take over the previous bitter zone. We're starving after unpacking, so I light the stove and tear into our stash of Amy's refried beans and corn. Feb opens a new package of flour tortillas. We eat in silence. I know Feb though. My baby born in a snowstorm. The storm of a century beat down on our beach town while we were warm and cozy inside the hospital. She's scared right now. Which means she's probably determined to shut the world out and trap herself in her head. My therapist says to give her space. Like cookies on a sheet.

"I'm tired, Mom. Gonna go take a nap before I unpack some more."

Wouldn't she want to explore the property more? I mean it's only a quarter-acre lot, but still. *No Maria. She's eighteen and over it.* I hear my sister's quick-to-judge voice.

"Okay. Just put your new sheets on your bed, okay?" I tap her dresser the way people do when they're sending someone off in a taxi.

What a gorgeous young woman who knows not even a shred of her power and her worth. My snowstorm baby.

February

Charlene, my therapist, thinks I should practice expressing myself to Dax in third person over email. Tell them the story of what I am going through since they are the only person I trust. She thinks third person will help me "observe" and detach from some of my worries and stress over my dad being gone. She thinks it might help to "frame" my situation better so that I can make good choices for myself. Charlene says I'm eclipsed by false narratives about myself and the way I love (or don't love) and engage, and that it's fogging me up. She refuses to say *fucking me up,* even though I know it's the same thing. She thinks I am much stronger than I know. I think she's full of shit, but I promised her I'd at least try. I like rules and this third-person thing feels like a rule.

Third person emails to Dax...Check.

Charlene is full of crap...Check.

Stronger than I realize...Check.

Dad left because he was bored with us...Check.

Maria

Two days later and one or two boxes opened, we agree to go for a long walk down Bellethorn to see what's what. I know Feb would rather go to the vinyl store or the library downtown, but for now, we need fresh air. Maybe we'll bond over stray cats and plan how to rescue them over time. As if suddenly Feb will crave a do-gooder lifestyle, like we're in a movie.

Only a few other homes besides ours make up the neighborhood. Most are cedar-shingled and only a few are ancient vinyl like ours.

"I'm not making new friends. I told you that, Mom. I told you back home, and I don't want to tell you again," she said. She laces up and we head out the door.

"This is home now, and I know. It's just a walk. People are good, Feb. Not your father, but people are," I said. The thought of returning to our sunshine-dreams life made me dizzy, like I was spinning in circles rather than shifting the direction forward.

"Dax is enough. You are enough," she replied. She picks up the pace, clearly annoyed at my mere presence.

Now is not the time to argue with her. We're just going for a walk down our lush block. Mature poplars and oaks tower the edge of the streets and honeysuckle bushes overstay their welcome. Grass is overgrown in every direction between wildflowers and broken wooden fences. I spray our ankles with tick spray. Two houses down, so about half a mile away, there's a girl about Feb's age who's opening her mailbox in a pair of black shorts and a Journey T-shirt. I hide a smile as tightly as humanly possible.

Charlene

I wish I could say February is going through something, that new adult thing—the space where she's finished with high school and uncertain of her next decision in life, but that's too easy. That's not all it is, but a sliver of the stew happening in her head. She has major trust issues, and though Maria tries, in her own way, to be real with her, she's not affirming enough. There's always a hint of judgment from what Feb tells me. And what mother doesn't emit those hints? Mine did. But some don't.

I take it back. Some don't, and especially with all Feb has been through with the divorce and her father's new family. Maria could learn gentler language from what Feb has revealed to me. Validate Feb's fears over friendships and meeting new people. She could also throw a little bit of sugar on Feb's love of old cars, maybe bond some over the hobby she may not understand but chooses to support. That wouldn't hurt. Some days I wish Feb would bring her mom to the last ten minutes of the session. So far, she's not interested.

As for February's behavior towards her mother, she can tone the bitch-fest down a bit. If she shows her mom more trust, Maria may be responsive and understand Feb more. Trust could open some doors. This relationship has some serious potential for a real partnership as they both adjust to life in Lampton. Which I truly believe was the right move for this mother-daughter pair. The move will be their first passageway to healing. Feb mentioned her mom was reading Emma Remphro's memoir. God, Emma was a prude in grad school. But she does write a solid narrative with practical applications.

Third-person expression to Dax is Feb's homework. I solidly believe in trying new modes and exercises until my patient finds the one that feels right for them. It might surprise her. She didn't seem too obstinate about it, but if I know Feb, she'll try it once and then get bored. Or bitch about how tedious it feels. Or how she shouldn't have homework.

Wow, maybe I should trust Feb more.

February

"I'm Redd. Nice to meet you. You're the newbies, yes?" She had a face full of freckles and a head full of black curls. I looked to my mom, knowing she'd answer for us. Mom nodded and repositioned her glasses. This girl has shit on her mind, that I pick up on. I know it too well. The twisted expression that can only mean you know who you *want* to be, but never really reach the pinnacle of that version because you get in your own way every time.

"I'm Maria. This is Feb," she said, motioning her head to me. Redd gulped the water from her bottle that she brought out to check the mail. Probably in the middle of a workout or something. I'd never seen such defined calf muscles in my life. A total athlete as much as I was a car-magazine junkie.

"Yes. We're new," I uttered. She eyed us for a few seconds. I heard my voice, thick and awkward. "From down the shore." Ick. Who cares?

"Nice tans. I'm jealous. I'm sort of allergic to the sun," Redd said, her head bowed to the dirt pathway. It made me relate to her way more than if she looked us directly in the eyes. It tells me she isn't the life of the party. No one *really* likes the life of the party. It's a myth.

"Really?" Mom asked. Mom pulls on her tee to make sure her thick waist isn't visible.

"Mom. She's kidding. You're kidding, right? About the sun?" She thinks we're pathetic. She has to. Mom *and* daughter. Next, she'll expect us to drop off a fucking cracker-crusted casserole.

"I am. I like the shade. Winter girl here." I prayed my mom wouldn't bring up the fact that I was born in a snowstorm and named after the coldest month of the year. "Give me your number, Feb. I'll show you the best places in Lampton," she said. There it was. I knew she'd stop being relatable. But then again, we weren't pathetic in her mind after all.

"My cell is broken," I said, only for my mom to jab me with her elbow.

"Suit yourself, Feb. Nice to meet you guys." Redd walked back to her house with her bundle of mail without a second look backwards. My mother's heart was probably more broken than before our walk. It broke because of my dad. I'm just filling in.

Maria

If my daughter refuses friendship, love, whatever, I don't have it in me to force her. Besides, she helps me every afternoon with inventory and sales over at Yesterday's Trove. She checks the incoming magazines, constantly hoping for some paper friends. That I notice. That I am certain of. Her and those 1964 Chevys. At least Bob gave her something to hold on to. I catch her eyeing the old issues of *Life* too. Why she can't find some online interest group who also loves those things too is beyond me. She's never been proud enough of her unique hobbies. Instead, she Pine-Sols the store restroom and wipes the display cases with the blue ammonia.

February

I know Mom wants more for me. More interactions, less Pine-Sol, but I'm good. I promise her I will grab some takeout coffees at the café in Downtown Lampton. I risk running into people my age, but Mom begged me. Brigg's Coffee Barn has navy blue walls covered in canvases and metal things. And as expected, Redd is at a back table with a steaming cup of something in one hand and a sketchbook opened in front of her on the table. I order our almond milk lattes at the counter covered in local-business decals, and I hear Redd's voice over Adele's version of "Love Song." The crowd is all under the age of thirty from what I can tell.

"Feb. Come here." Direct and cutting, impossible to ignore. She's camped out in the back of the café beneath two canvases—one dripping in black hearts over a sword, and one with a vase of plum azaleas…or maybe peonies?

I pay for my cups and head over to Redd, hoping it'll be brief and easy to wiggle out of. She's ultra zoned-in on whatever's on her sketchpad which is now tilted and facing her, not me or anyone else.

"Can I see?" I ask, thinking it's a natural question for someone with a sketchpad and a look in her eye. She's tapping her pencil, and her tea is releasing lemon tones everywhere.

"Sure. In a minute." She rotates the pad horizontally as if it makes a difference in her own approval of her work. She erases a spot and shades something in, I assume. I know nothing about art and drawing, so shade and color, it's all the same to an onlooker.

"What is it?" I ask, taking a sip of my latte before it gets to room temp. I like it steaming so that I'm forced to savor and not slurp. Why do I care so much? This isn't supposed to be the case. I'm failing at failing at friendship. Damn it.

"You know what? How about you guess?" She smirks, and for some reason it pisses me off. She carefully sips her tea, never releasing my gaze.

"I don't know anything about you. Except that you look like an athlete. Is it a soccer ball?" I squirm in my seat.

She laughs and shakes her head. "This is very true. You know nothing about me. At all. Two more guesses. I'm not athletic at all. It's just genetics. My legs, right?"

I blush and nod, feeling mortified. "Then I don't know. A guitar? A bowl of fruit?" I stare above her head at the black hearts and sword, totally embarrassed.

"Ha! No. But I appreciate your effort. It's the most you've made in the week you've been here."

"What's that supposed to mean?" I know what it means. It means I haven't even tried to be a human being who's eighteen years old in a new place.

"It means you never come out of your house, or if you do, it's to work with your mom. You know everyone our age hangs here or down by the horse farm. I know you know it."

"Whatever. I don't need more friends. Mine is up in Buffalo, but they're coming in the fall."

"Yeah…it's July, Feb." She drops a teaspoon of honey into her mug.

"Look, I didn't ask to come over here. I—" I try to leave, but she's not having it.

"Wait." She stands up and reaches for my hand. "I'm sorry. I just think…I think we are more alike than you realize. But you have to want to realize. Make sense?"

I sit back down. She's good at this. "I guess." At that, she turns the sketchbook in my direction and my heart drops. My heart drops because it's the most beautiful broken heart under a pair of sad eyes. I have never seen something in pencil like it. Like I could feel it. Like she drew something alive. I can't speak. The things I don't know how to do—the lines, shadows, whatever, are so accurate and so...breathing. But I am not.

"I know heartache too," Redd said, looking me straight in my sad eyes. The hurt in her face is soft but real.

Shit. I do want a friend.

CHARLI

Charli zeroed in on Robben's Pink Floyd T-shirt. It was a Sherwin Williams-leaning-toward-brown taupe base with their band logo across the front in chunky yellow font. She bought it for him from one of those band T-shirt pop-ups online. Charli married Robben five years ago because he promised equality and charcuterie Fridays. She loved the olives. They met at a writers' conference in New York one winter, and it was a really slow courtship, but a thrilling one. They both attended a panel on Fantasy in YA and commented on how much the genre had grown. Everything clicked—from the sex, to the conversation, to the food. He never gave her a hard time about her bad habits, like eating in bed or pulling the cheese off her pizza, except near the edge of the crust. He never gave her a hard time about much, and though it reads like a dream come true, it was leaning toward stale.

Up until this second of summer, the togetherness of the two of them, every Friday—cheese, meats, and documentaries about the food they were eating, and once in a while, the art of repurposing old furniture, felt good. Charli loved Robben, she did. He treated her truly as his equal partner, but as she zeroed in on that T-shirt, the air felt like a blank index card, except for the trees which induced dollops of magic that landed in her drink only. The air though—no lines. No notes. Clean and empty. She claimed she had always wanted a life of peace and tranquility, but peace and tranquility can often crush the chaos that sustains desire.

Questions jumped out of the fire-pit embers. "Where's the tension in this chapter? Why doesn't Charli want to jump Robben and feel his face on hers?" He kept his every promise, fixed every sloppy chip in the pavement and walls of their journey. All the way from Boston, where they had settled after their wedding, to West Hartford, CT, where they now worked for separate publishers. Boston started to feel too noisy, so when they explored the opportunities in WH, they found it had a downtown that was much quieter but still enough for their needs. Plus, more affordable. Robben loved it immediately, but Charli grew fonder by the day once Blue Star Books opened its doors and she had a place to comb for classics.

The leaves on the ground winked at Charli. She picked one up and crumbled it over the fire as Robben refilled the cheddar and Kalamatas. She rarely had to lift a finger. It was everything most women aspire to, actually. When Charli needed a hand with her lumpy edits, Robben left his pile of manuscript slush to help her. He was a talented editor, maybe more than her, but he'd never express that. He allowed her the spotlight where she belonged. Even that felt dim now.

"Rhett and Jilly arrive at around ten tomorrow," Robben told Charli as he offered her a thin triangle of cheese and a steel toothpick. He had no clue about her indifference this mild summer evening.

"Okay. Do we have to pick them up, or are they renting a car?" Charli asked, words linear, with a delicate sip of her mojito.

She dreaded the pretend of the next few days with their guests. The "Here we all are, together again, as high-powered couples" pretend poses.

It used to be real. Charli and Jilly would run a few miles in the morning before they all had coffee and bagels, while Robben and Rhett would listen to Van Halen on vinyl. Then they'd all go to the farmers' market, maybe grab a few beers and tapas downtown, and then they'd nap before a late dinner in their backyard by the pool. Maybe it would still feel real for the three of them. When Rhett and Jilly moved to Cleveland, things fizzled everywhere. In the trees, in the house, and in the whole marital cosmos. A leaf trickled off the backyard poplar as Charli sipped again. She watched its journey onto the concrete, in awe of its freedom.

"No. They're renting a Zip. What's up, sweetheart? You're...I don't know. On Mars or something?" Robben asked.

"I'm just tired. That Pressman deadline was rough." She readjusted her legs on her Adirondack chair. She twiddled the white fringy string on her cover-up.

"Sirloin or veal for tomorrow night? Personally, I'm craving a Piccata," Robben said, his right dimple miles deep.

"Whichever," Charli sighed and cleared her throat.

Charli faded into the crisp summer sound of Sting coming out of their very expensive speakers. She could be in Charleston by tomorrow night. Get some perspective. Find some new artists for her publisher. Maybe meet up for coffee with an old friend who happened to live there. Charleston was where Charli met her employer only a few years ago at a conference. It was also where her high-school sweetheart, Sean, lived.

Robben turned up the volume on his beloved grainy Doors song when they came up on the shuffle and disappeared into himself and his martini. Charli didn't mind. It gave her permission to continue the same for a while. Jim Morrison was not her idea of meditation, but the shuffle usually considered the interest of both parties in equal doses.

"Veal Piccata does sound good," she said. "Buy the good lemons."

"Great. I'll grab the stuff tomorrow before they arrive," Robben said and winked at her.

"Honey…if I took off for a few days, would you be upset?" She stared at the leaf on the ground, holding strong in her choice to remain still.

"I knew something was up," he said as he skimmed the deep end of the pool.

"Nothing's up. I just need a breather from work, from here. Not from you." She winked back at Robben, but his face said he didn't totally buy it. She found his strong shoulders and triceps with her eyes and remembered how he kissed. Like he meant it.

The poplar lost another leaf. Two sides of the same leaf with very different tones. Duplicitous. Charli picked up the leaf, this time not crumbling it, but twisting it between her fingers. Exploring its duality. The leaf felt feminine mostly, with a glaze of masculinity hiding in its seed. Its veins.

"Not from you. I love you," she said, her eyes on the leaf. Her eyes seared into the contradiction of the leaf.

***

The first day with their friends went exactly as it always had. Jogs, fresh local honey, and salmon on the cedar plank and grill. They had spent the second day hiking, eating plant-based sushi, and laughing. Nothing unusual about their visit, and that was Charli's precise qualm. Charli left for Charleston the morning after Rhett and Jilly left for home. She told Robben that Charleston was simply to gain some fresh takes for her growing client list. To sort her head—like Kate Beckinsale says in *Serendipity* when she runs away to New York to do the same thing, when secretly she feels John Cusack's character in her path. In her air.

Charleston was supposed to be good for the stagnant spirit, according to an article Charli read online from a blog for publishing professionals. Apparently Charleston was oozing with colors and feels. Someone clearly made that up in an attempt to boost their tourism, as every city in the world oozes with those things. Almost every city. Charli's personal favorite was Québec, but her passport wasn't updated. Charleston would give Charli the perspective she needed about her relationship with Robben. She'd know if she still loved him when she boarded the plane home. That was two days from now.

She packed a ton of her beloved Anjou pears and boarded her flight to Charleston, South Carolina. She leaned her head on the small flight pillow and remembered how she'd wished for a marriage that was easy and light. She'd wished for it, yet here she was. The flight was smooth, except for the sniffling teenager behind her. Sniff, sniff. *Oh my God, blow your nose, already,* Charli thought.

Upon arrival, Charli had to use the airport bathroom, so she scrubbed hands afterward as if she was exiting a surgery, and then splashed her face. The agitation had two sides, like that poplar leaf. Internal doubt about what she wanted and annoyance at the teen that needed a tissue.

Check in at the Madras Inn wasn't until 3 p.m. and it was only noon, so she had time to browse the Charleston gift boutiques that she read about on a blog—all of the soy candles and designer matchbooks anyone could ask for along with ropes, birchwood, and notebooks as if they were made in a barn in a rural town and shipped over. Barn-to-display-table—rosemary and sage sprigs sprinkled randomly, but not chaotic. And then buyer's remorse when you realize you can't recreate the woodsy-ethereal-textural vibe at home. And you just spent twelve dollars on a matchbook because of the artwork on the front, all Tuscan and rich.

Madeline's Reach was the first boutique. She pictured the person she came here for because it wasn't the blog. It was Sean. He'd moved to Charleston five years ago, and they had exchanged a few emails over the years. The tiny sliver he occupied in her heart had grown as she and Robben became more of a question mark. Only Robben had no idea about these mixed-up feelings. As Charli browsed the shop she texted Robben to check in with him. He didn't answer her. Her text was marked as read, but he didn't reply to her *I'm here. Miss you. All good?* It rubbed her wrong. She panicked a bit inside. What if he was meeting up with Beth, his high- school sweetheart? She breathed in an orange-seed candle and exhaled to a count of six.

Publishing had jaded her a bit, and that was okay. She'd rather spend her money on books than these lavender sachets and tea caddies. So many books. This store had a shelf full of books about botanicals and barns. Did Sean buy gifts here? Did he even know these stores existed in his city?

Charli checked into her inn by 3:45 p.m. and immediately sent Sean the email. She was here. It had been what? Twelve years since they had seen one another. About that. She showered and moisturized and only glazed a layer of peach gloss on her lips and a dab of mascara on her eyes.

Their emails over the years were innocent enough, carrying no scent of yearning or *I miss you so much.* They were just check-ins. *How have you been? Hope you are well. Did you see the new* Coming 2 America*?*

He was already at the highly recommended seafood restaurant behind a magazine about cheese and culture. “Hi, Charli. You look beautiful. Like always.” Charli blushed. Then pressed her lips together. She sat down, careful not to knock the glass of water over, as she was trembling. Inside. Hopefully not noticeable on the exterior.

“It’s you.” She sipped. He sipped. They chatted for hours over lobster bisque, oyster crackers, and the most delicious shrimp cocktail she’d ever eaten. White wine for her. Sparkling water for Sean. Charli was aware of every facial twitch she made, every gesture, every word to the wait staff. Her lips felt detached, and her heart was unstoppable. She felt some guilt too.

“Charli,” he said and touched her hand. “I’m experimenting with something.” Charli flinched. It’s probably something like popping balloons during sex. It’s too bad because he looked so great with gray hair and some forehead lines. Maybe it wasn’t balloons, but instead he’s trying out a vegan lifestyle, but also one void of sugar and all things delicious?

He proceeded to tell her about his end-of-intimacy journey. No more women. No more sex. He had been heartbroken and soul-broken too many times. And it began with her, fifteen years ago. Charli held in her dinner. Tight and wrapped up in whatever goes on inside those organs. If she acknowledged how she wanted to vomit from his words, she would have spewed everywhere.

She collapsed alone on her Queen bed at the Madras Inn. She crawled under the covers, shut the light, and cried herself to sleep. She’d get on the first plane home tomorrow. Her view was clear. Relationships shift. Relationships never remain the same. As much as we want them to. Or not.

Before getting on the flight back to Hartford, Charli dropped back into Madeline's Reach and bought Robben a twelve-dollar matchbook. The one with a painted pear on it. Maybe mocking the boutiques artisanal selection was bad Karma, so she had to course-correct.

She grabbed her window seat on the flight home, taking bite after bite of her last Anjou.

She knew she loved those pears, and that was all she knew.

NINA

The recessed lights blind me, as if I'm on Blue Conch Beach at 11 a.m. The dimmer switch of the adjoining family room lights strikes at full blast shoved to the top notch. Head spins, but I am physically standing still, and I notice that no one else is fazed by these obnoxious Los Angeles recessed lights. They're like Gilbert Gottfried reincarnated. Screaming at me with giant teeth and annoying sounds, telling me to get over myself. "NINA. What's your problem? HEH? Lights bother you? What else is NEW?"

Sweaty neck, itchy chin, lumpy throat. More sweat, like I just biked to and from the diner a mile away, shoveled a full stack of pancakes down my throat, repeating the task twenty times. Enough to provoke a cocktail of reflux and nausea. My head whips around as if on that rusty rollercoaster that everyone insists is a local treasure. It's a piece of shit is what it is. I grab some girl's arm, but she shrugs away, thinking I am going to vomit on her. She sees the swivel in my eyes. *Get away from me, you freak,* she thinks. *Go bother someone who cares.* I can't really argue with that look.

I sprint straight to the bathroom, afraid I'll throw up all over this very white house marked at every few feet with vases and Lladró figurines from the late 1980s. Nothing comes up my esophagus, but there I am, kneeling over the toilet, trying to conjure up images of a peaceful horse in a field in September. The farm my dad loved so much. Apples strewn about. Dandelions smiling. I coax myself back to calm. It works, but I know my time is limited before the next wave of whatever this is. Needles in my eyes. Pavers on my chest. *Shut up, you know what it is.* My gut tosses in circles. Early Black Sabbath beats in my temple.

Somatic anxiety, I remember reading about it when it started a few years ago. The pain ball would roll from my sinuses to my armpit to my calves. Like a pinball machine triggered by something as small as the mention of the word destiny.

I sneak into the very shiny dining room, where nobody is now. It's pouring outside.

"Nina, what is going on with you right now?" a friend probes with his signature compassion. I know him well. He was hiding behind the hutch staring at his cigarette. He was there for me at every turn, with his songs and his piano. Like he was really there with me. "You're okay. It's okay." He rubs my back as I lean on an oversized dining room chair the color of dark chocolate. For weeks, back in the doldrums of January, it was he who met me in the graveyard in our town's cemetery to visit our classmates who'd lost lives in the boardwalk fire when we were in tenth grade. It was he who'd find me sulking over sheet music in an empty lesson room because my panic attack prevented me from blowing even a single note out of my trombone at rehearsal. It was he who knew when to put a hand on my shoulder by my locker in between classes. I was having a flare up of this same problem today. Every turn.

"Maybe it was a bad piece of iceberg?" I say. "It seemed kind of wilty," I moan. He knows what it is, but he simply rubs my back without judgment. Because I think he's like me. Wilty iceberg?

That's weak. "I'll be fine. I'm heading home. I don't want a scene," I say. My hand grips his forearm while I breathe deeply and adjust my feet on the floor, grounding myself again. I wait to call on them. I imagine the horse again. Red delicious apples. Yellow candy-bright flowers. Alright, fine. It's time. I ask for help from La Stregheria that streams through my blood. They seem to be hearty saviors when I need them to step in, their nails and eyelashes the size of Saturn, their veins pumping with answers.

The thunder outside has softened. Then, a collective gasp from the kitchen regarding the lightning streak through the very white window treatments. The power in the house fizzled and drained from every bulb. I heard Lily Stratford shriek out of fear. Carly Mason let out a giant "Fuck me!" because it's her house and now she has to manage the crowd in her living room. My witches love the dark, so locating me wouldn't be stressful like the time at the fifth-grade End-of-Year picnic, midday. To be honest, I have no clear knowledge about their process and how they arrive.

"Are you going to be okay, Nina?" my friend asks. I can tell he's being polite. I swear he's like me but hasn't found the courage to express it yet. Then again, neither have I.

"I will be." I manage a hug and hold it for a few seconds. "I'll see you later?" I say it to his neck, still unable to release him.

I convince him to stay at Carly's house while I walk home with heavy eyes. It feels good to cry now because it's been a while. The torrential rain refreshes my skin and stomps on my anxious body. It's hot rain. Sobbing in hot, suburban rain must be what it's like to belt out tragic opera. Defiance and balance at just the right temperature.

It's only 7:30 p.m., but I lie on my back with my eyes closed, a monster headache pounding at my temples, Sabbath gone, and the ceiling fan on high. I grabbed a towel from the hall closet to put under my wet head because that argument with Mom is zero fun: "You'll make mold!" she'd insist. La Stregheria respected the dynamic between my mother and me, but also chose sides when some of her habits proved unreasonable. I think they empathized with my struggle. This struggle. This thing that my brain can't talk itself out of.

The swivel and clink of the fan chain is comforting. The Kelly-green fringe on the fan pull is a soft focal point. I wait. I thank La Stregheria for getting me home safely. Knowing it's time to tell people who I am. Dead once. Back again on a mission, reborn. Queen of something. Friend to all. Enemy to those who bite.

FEATHER IN FIRST

They totally forget to mention that the thing you look forward to most loses all thrill and shimmer by the time it arrives. You've gotten over it before it even begins. Enter, The Senior Car Scramble of Cedar North. Basically, every senior stands by the driver side of their car. The senior class advisors blow obnoxious whistles and we run around like maniacs all over the parking lot, not knowing when those whistles will be blown again. When the whistle blows again, the car we're standing closest to is the car we get to baptize using neon foamy string and whatever other harmless, easy-to-clean things we managed to sneak in our pockets. It's dumb, but it's highly regarded, and the actual fun part is the part seniors added about a decade ago. That part consists of making out with the classmate whose car you land on. But if they're elsewhere you find them in your travels and give them a big old French kiss for the records. As the years progressed, seniors learned to squat out of sight of our advisors. The advisors added juniors to the mix, keeping the flow moving so that people didn't hunt down their friends' cars instead of sticking with the task at hand. I forgot to mention that every senior has a pre-made cardboard sign with their name spray painted on it so that if we weren't familiar with the car, we'd still know whose car we landed on. To further complicate things, everyone wears a bandana around their mouth and nose for mystique. Yep. The Senior Car Scramble, complete with coffee thermoses full of Gatorade and vodka for most, rum and Coke for others. All I was packing was a peppermint wheel on my tongue for the lucky guy or girl.

It lost its luster before it even started, and I know it's because of Tim. I'd rather be with him and his friends. I was over my Cedar Northers. No wonder I'm in the middle of nowhere all the time. I can never be where I am. Sandra Golden has her freckled arm around me and tells me she loves me and will miss me and how band would never have been so much fun without our friendship. And still, I feel nothing. I'm a terrible person to have detached on the day I'm still needed by people as sweet as Sandra. I force a smile and kiss her cheek. She knows I forced it. She walks away toward Laurel Miller, and I can't blame her. Emotional dissonance feels like garbage on the receiving end.

"Feather, I feel bad for you. You're going to regret it one day, being so *whatever* you are right now. Removed, I think? Eddie is right," she said before she's totally out of earshot.

"Great. Eddie's team." So over it all. "Love you too! Have fun!"

She rolls her eyes at me, shrugs, and joins Laurel, ass in full swing for Billy Ginquist, class clown but also class expert in the thing all girls love: oral sex.

I land on Mike Jenson's car, squiggle nonsense all over his Toyota with two full cans of pink string, holding back a smile. He's someone I could deal with kissing—those feathery eyelashes and salty surfer skin, but I doubt I'll bring myself to it. One, because Tim's kisses are still swimming in my memory, and two, because Eddie and Mike are tight.

I find out fast that his friendship with Eddie didn't hold a ton of weight.

Mike's behind me with one hand on my shoulder. "Feath. Let's do this," he whispers in my ear. "God, I've always wanted you," he says as we both drop in sync to our knees on the pavement. I turn to face him. I wore a long maxi dress and thank God because I was having an extra bloat kind of day. "Seriously."

"Mike Jenson, come on. You love Kate," I tousle his hair and touch his face. He grabs my hand quicker than I expect and laces his fingers in mine. "Mike. Seriously?" We rip off our bandanas.

"Feather. Disappear from this street, our town, this school for a minute," he says and twirls his fingers around mine. It tickles me a bit in every nerve ending. My other hand drops onto his bended denim knee. I notice it's not just his eyelashes that overthrow me, but his very defined Adam's apple. "Put your hand on me."

"Where?" I know what he means by the crumble of his voice on me. The needy slur of me. "Mike … I …" I am frozen in this place in time, terrified to look him in the eye. I can't hear anything else. I can't see anything else but his lips. I slide my hand over his crotch and leave it there, watching, waiting. He puts his hand on my inner thigh.

We sit, breathe. I feel him pulling in closer. "Oh, I'm so serious Feather Sierra," he says, eyelashes five miles long. "Ever since sophomore history. You and that damn neck," he said. Oh, that's right. He liked my neck, of all things. "What would Madonna do right now?" Oh, I didn't love that. To be honest he almost had me before exploiting the incomparable Queen of Pop to me.

"So, to be clear, you're Team Feather, then?" I say, aware that I have ruined the intense moment. I jammed myself in the middle of nowhere once again. Boner killer.

"Dude. Why? You know I think Eddie's an ass most of the time," he said. Our hands are no longer interlaced or on each other or anywhere near that yearn, and I know if I say the right thing, I could have his lips close to mine again.

"I'm just...I don't know...wondering." I take his hand back in mine but he resists.

"I was as hard as a rock, but now I'm kind of...not." Damn it, Feather.

"UGH. I'm sorry. It's just—"

"Listen to me closely, Feather," he says, all friendship zoney and direct, with his hands gently wrapped around my wrists. "Leave Cedar and don't come back for a year. You've earned it. Eddie can't shake you if you come back around. So you have to shake him. For good."

"Really? This is how you feel?" I ask. "He's leaving too. Even further than me."

"It's how we all feel, Feath. You're making him crazy with this new guy," Mike aid.

"Good to know," I said and kissed him on the cheek in a no big deal kind of way, but still slowly so he knows I wanted him too. In some other lifetime.

"Wait," he says and pulls me back down from the loudness into our little almost sex nook. "In five years, on July fourth, if you are alone and single, meet me right here. And we can pick up where we almost took off," he said.

"Are you serious?" I asked.

"Very."

"Deal."

***

"So Mike Jenson is way hotter than I ever gave him credit for," I said as soon as I divvied up the crackers between Kelsey and me. "We almost made out. Speaking of, I didn't see you."

"Oh my God, Feather. One guy at a time. You're gonna give Eddie a massive heart attack," she said. "I skipped and met Dan at his house. We did it twice," she said.

"Oh. Good for you. Safely, yes?" I asked and scoured our fridge for the fresh package of deli American, rather than the plastic bag with bits and corners left. Mom hated when I opened a new one before finishing the old, but I didn't care. "Why am I responsible for Eddie's well-being, by the way?"

"Good point, and of course we were safe," Kelsey answered. "I don't need a baby in the middle of Virginia." Kelsey would begin James Madison University in the fall. And of course, instead of a standard dorm room she'd have a cushy apartment off campus.

Mid-cracker, our house phone rang. It was Tim. "Hey! Are you still coming by to get me?" He told me he'd be by in twenty minutes, and we'd go to the boardwalk. My face was on fire and Kelsey rolled her eyes at the glimpse of my pelvic thrusting to make her laugh. She laughed too, but nevertheless, rolled her eyes as well.

Ten crackers with cheese later, we hear Tim's car pull up. Kelsey waved to him, hugged me, and rode her bike home. She had to share her car with her twin brother, Bryce, so he had dibs today. "Don't forget. One day of school left," she whispered in my ear.

"One day." I inhale dusk and the smell of our neighbor's charcoal grill.

"Kelsey! HEY!" Tim rolled his window down and yelled. She gave him a wave from behind her head; she was already halfway down the street. She was not nearly as social as me. Which was fine. One good look at her legs and straight brown hair, and I had to worry with every guy I dated. As harmless as Kelsey came across, she had it in her to betray me if she really dug deep enough. That made me sad, but I've known it since we were in second grade, and she stole Steven Pertinari from me. I didn't talk to her for two weeks. She apologized with an amazing unicorn eraser that we ended up burying on the side of my house. We swore we'd dig it up when we were eighty years old.

"Lover, give me your face," Tim said, motioning for me to kiss him through the car window. I knew something was up already. This date wasn't happening. He wasn't as wrapped up in me as I was in him this early on. I knew it. God, he smelled like a guy in summer—seashells, strawberries, with a hint of citrus in his mouth. We kissed so wet, and I drowned. I was totally in love.

"Listen, I had to pick up an extra shift at work. One of the waiters called out, and I owe him anyway. I could use the cash too," he said, grazing his fingers from my collarbone to my eyebrows. "I'm so sorry to bail like this. Tomorrow night?"

"I mean it's graduation, so?" I shrugged.

"Oh, shit! It is, isn't it? Well, I could come by here. Are you guys having a party or something?" He sounded eager to do that, so this was a better sign. He also had this wrecked way about him. Not so groomed, and very street smart. This being another giant difference between Cedar North and Cedar South. Another reason I didn't love being on the North side of the team. Yet, likely the South would find me too North. Even in this tiny crumb of the Earth, I fell in the in between.

"Just family, but yes. Come by," I said and bit his bottom lip gently, first making sure my parents were nowhere in sight. "Oh, how was your prom? I heard you went with Stacy Van Alls?"

His face dropped, but he picked it up fast, and my stomach fell into itself. Never a good sign. "Yeah…uh…it was okay. She's cool and all." He totally hooked up. I wanted to vomit.

"Why just okay?" I wasn't going to let this go away easily. I know how he answered because it's how I answered when Eddie asked me how my "date" was with a band senior I saw a movie with during the first week of dating Eddie. I did kiss him close-mouthed goodbye when he dropped me off afterwards. Now Tim is serving up my karma.

"Crap. I'm gonna be late. Listen. You're amazing. Good luck tomorrow. I know you have a speech to give and all," he said. Eyes paired with arm hair paired with sweat. I could barely stand after this last kiss. He was on fire in ways I couldn't relate to. Kids from Cedar South weren't as entitled and privileged, and so they had a special drive for life at its most, I don't know…honest? "I'll see you tomorrow. How's six?"

"Awesome. Bye." He pulled away. I was positive he hooked up at prom. Eddie would be thrilled. I stood watching his mom's clunky Oldsmobile putter down my street. He watched me watch him through the mirror. Barefoot, denim jean shorts, in the middle of nowhere, feeling teamless and undevoted to anyone. As usual.

When Eddie and I were in the thick of our relationship I knew I'd break his heart.

"I can never imagine kissing anyone else," he'd say in the darkness of his basement with my hair cascading all over his face.

"Ever?" I'd ask without a tone attached to it because I couldn't choose one.

"Never." That was our first Christmas together, and along with my hair dangling in his face was the silver necklace he picked out and wrapped for me. I still have the heart. And likely his too, except that Eddie's heart is in chunky pieces all over Cedar.

As I stepped on my porch, I noticed a paper rectangle on one of my dad's matured juniper bushes. It was a playing card of sorts, but with a detailed illustration in pencil of a woman with flowing hair. Under her face were the words: *Isolt, Undying Love.* My instinct was first to turn it over to find a blank side, and then to smell it. It smelled like patchouli. Louis? Definitely not Kelsey. I crammed it in my pocket after folding it in half and headed upstairs for a thousand pleas to work off my new American-cheese gut.

FEBRUARY AND COMPANY

February

We have one week until the annual downtown Lampton Scarecrow Contest, and all Redd and I have completed is the stuffing of Eddie's boots and pants. My old beach town was far too disjointed to pull of any kind of contest, as it was spread out into sections. The downtown thing makes me happy now, and I don't miss the ocean the way I thought I would. She swears to me Eddie Van Halen is the way to go. With his passing, she thinks it's the most killer way to pay tribute to one of the best rock guitarists ever. Her words, not mine. I wouldn't know a good guitar player if he or she kicked me in the face. I mean, "Panama" is a cool song, but I can't decipher chords or anything like she can.

As I eye the progress, something in me switches gears.

"This is all wrong. We need a new idea. Sorry, Eddie." Redd glares at me with eyes as sharp as the straw all over our clothes.

"Oh no. No, no, no. We planned it all out. We agreed Prince was too purple, and David Bowie too predictable."

"Why does it have to be a man, and why do they have to be dead?"

"I mean, I didn't think it *had* to be a man. You didn't offer any suggestions, so I just thought—"

"You didn't ask me for any!" I didn't mean to sound so aggressive about it, but she was being so nonchalant as she began Eddie's shirt and arm stuffing to create an upper torso.

"Well, it's a team situation, so for you to offer your suggestion would not have offended me, Feb." She wiped her forehead from the hot October midday sun. "I'm not married to the idea, but Eddie seemed like a cool one, you know?"

"Eh. I'm not sold, and I wish I'd said something sooner," I say under my breath, but apparently not quietly enough.

"It's too late now. Suck it up, buttercup." The words cut through my face, all the way to my toes, and I hate it. They came out of her mouth gently, like taffy, but still. Something in me snaps. I drop my part of the scarecrow and storm away. Like a child. She doesn't call or chase after me, and that part is hard as I pass the bakery, then the library. I made a friend, and here I am screwing it up.

Maria

I met someone named Ralph. I like him, Feb likes him, and he likes us. We met while standing in line at the Lampton Hardware store. Feb was at Redd's house, and my arms were full of paint cans because I'd forgotten a shopping cart. I planned on only a few sample cans of Soft Purple but ended up going a little overboard with so many shades to choose from. Ralph grabbed the wooden stirrers that toppled off my piles of cans cradled in my arms. He was very sweet from the beginning, and with no pretense about him.

"You look like you need a shopping cart, though I think you can make it. You're only one person away from the register," he said, handing me my stirrers. We've been spending almost every day together since. He visits me at the antique store, and Feb approves of his tacos. I think she's happy I'm off her case. The situation works. I still worry about Feb, though. Having Redd as a friend is a good thing, but I am deep-down afraid she's going to mess it up. If Redd makes one wrong move or says one wrong word, I fear he'll see Feb's worst quality—her lack of trust.

She came home earlier today and made a beeline to her bedroom. My fear might be in motion already. Ralph says there's only one way to know for sure—*ask her.* That's easier said than done. He never had kids. Married once briefly, but no children.

Feb is a closed book when she lets me in her room. I encourage her to call Charlene and set something up. She looks at me with her giant eyes that I'll forever see as if she's five, and my mama-bear heart disintegrates in my chest. My baby.

Charlene

Mistrust. Fear of abandonment. Flight over fight. Trauma responses. It was bound to happen to her eventually, but I think she's going to be okay. It also depends on how patient and empathetic her new friend is.

"Did you try and discuss this in detail? Or did you run?"

"I ran. Well, I walked, but yeah."

Something about Eddie Van Halen over a female icon? I see her point, but a friendship-ruiner it is *not.*

"Feb. Talk to her about it."

"I know."

She knows.

Feb

Dax asked me if I I'm being a little too sensitive. And when they used these words, *they* were sensitive. So how can I argue? Their exact words were, "Is there a chance you're being oversensitive about something you're not even that passionate about?"

I replied, "It's possible." But they're right. It's not about the scarecrow. I assumed the worst before I asked more questions. I flew away.

Redd wants to meet at her house in an hour. We have two days before the scarecrow contest if we mend this. I don't even know if I screwed up, or if I care, or if she cares. A lie—I care. Redd is the first friend I've ever had who isn't worried about what everyone around her thinks about her.

"You're late. Follow me." I do as she says, and we head toward her backyard, the moon poking through the evening's sky—a sliver tonight. She pauses at the gate with her hand on the latch. "Next time, let's talk. Walking away is bullshit, you know?"

"I get it," I say, eyes on the slice in the sky because it's a marvel against the navy tablecloth of the October sky.

Positioned on the back deck is the most outrageously stand-out scarecrow donned in a red-and-white laced, poofy skirt, yellow heels, and crazy pink hair. I recognize the thick purple belt because it belongs to Redd.

"Cyndi Lauper. Because why not?" She smiles. I want to cry.

Instead, I hug her tight and whisper, "I'm sorry I was an asshole to you."

"We're good. I get it. You're a rookie at this."

I'm a rookie and suddenly very awake. I swear the moon winks.

KATRINA

Katrina Stazio loved Miami Sound Machine. She found them years before the lead singer's name was included in the name of band. She blasted her CD from a portable player as she painted her fence—"Falling in Love (Uh-Oh)" echoed through the backyard, across her blue hydrangeas, way up to the top of her cucumber vines. It was something about Gloria's voice that connected to Katrina, who leaned romantic. In all areas of her life, from ice cream flavor to the color of her bedroom carpet, Katrina opted for romance. Butter Pecan and pale purple. Katrina cherished having summers off. Teaching was really the best profession for people who liked to complete large-scale projects in the summer, like gardening or painting murals on fences. The doughnut mural took up all of her time now, and she wouldn't have it any other way. It was inspired by her daughter, Clem, and her friends who begged for something cheerful and bright.

"Hi, Mom. What is this?" There was no build up, warm up, or prep time for Katrina to consider the question because her ten-year-old daughter Clem held the rosary necklace front and center over the peanut-butter-colored paint tray. No warning, only triggers. Katrina's stomach roiled at the sight of the spherical stones. "Mom, tell me! I love it." She twirled in joy as if the necklace was unearthed accompanied by a mound of loose gems and pirate gold. The rosary stones had a certain presence, like an all-knowing woman with strong cheekbones. Katrina didn't think her child would care so much, but here she fluttered, as Katrina fought to hold her lunch down. The beads incited riot in Katrina's bones.

"Where did you find it, Clementina? I haven't seen this in years." Katrina's heart beat with a rattle. She wiped her forehead with her shirt sleeve and panted from the heat. Or maybe it was an oncoming panic attack.

"Miss Kelly left it on my bed with a note. She found it under the sofa cushions in your library." Clementina was smiling because that was her trademark. She was the smile to her mom's gravity. The rainbow to Katrina's pale purple. Damn Miss Kelly for being the most proficient cleaning professional in the world.

"Oh. That makes sense." Katrina filled in the chocolate crème doughnut with brown paint to contrast its hot pink bakery box with a steady hand and an out-of-control pulse. Clementina promised her she would do the white shadowing to depict sheen and gloss. It was meant to be a mother-daughter project, after all.

"So what is it? It doesn't look like a necklace I would wear. Can I have it?" she screeched. Most people have seen or have some experience with rosaries, but Katrina knew Clem only had a couple of friends, all Jewish American. Rosaries weren't flowing in her homes or cars. Also growing up with Katrina's mantra—We believe in good and in each other, and in love—didn't shed any light on the necklace's meaning.

"They're called rosary beads. Gram Teresa gave them to me to give to you. I did when you were three, but you must've stuffed them into the couch, and I never thought to look for them." Katrina said it like she had rehearsed it for exactly seven years.

Like she knew the beads would eventually surface. Like a chip of eggshell in a cooked omelet—one dripping in salmonella.

Clementina placed the blue-green beads around her neck and pirouetted in between the trays of paints like the gemstone she has been since birth. She assumed a tree pose and tried to spark a smile in Katrina.

"Mama, talk to me. Tell me what to do with these sparkly spheres!"

Katrina couldn't help but smirk because she loved her daughter so much, but her body didn't budge from painter position—facing the fence, filling in the chocolate. Clem rebalanced her pose until it stuck.

"Listen, my sweet pea. Google rosary beads or ask someone when school starts. You know I don't like formal religion. Okay? It's not personal. It's what I kindly request of you. I love you." Katrina's grin vanished, and she moved on to the powdered jelly doughnut.

"I understand, Mom. I love you too. But look how when the sun hits them, they look like tropical water." Clementina switched legs in her tree pose and put her hands in Namaste. Life was a giant exclamation point for Clem. Everything a gift.

Katrina attended St. Benedicta when she was younger and never forgave the rough nature of Sister Rosemary. Apparently, Katrina asked too many questions and sparked too many discussions. Sister Rosemary called her "far too troublesome" to be considered a nice little girl. It was the reason the Stazios did not bring religion into their home. And Clementina was too curious for her own good. Katrina made certain that, without any church or formal instruction, they believed in each other, in love, and being good people. Sister Rosemary once yelled at Katrina for thinking she knew more than her just because her dad took her to Italy in the summers: "You know nothing. I am the teacher. You are the student. Italy was a waste of your time."

Gloria's voice faded as Katrina's memories got louder. Clem found the container of pink bubbles over by the marigold patch. With "Conga" barely audible and her daughter in love with life, Katrina sat on the rotted wooden bench under their walnut tree. It was 1958. Sister Rosemary asked the class to stop chatting even though they had just returned from the dining hall and were settling in for the rest of the afternoon. Arithmetic was next, but Katrina and her friends were wrapping up their conversation about the big kickball tournament after school. They'd planned it for weeks, sorting out teams, gathering designated ribbon color, and asking moms to contribute soda and snacks. It was a highly anticipated afternoon. Katrina's classmates had settled in, but for Ralph VelDiccio in the back right corner of the room who blurted a loud, "Can't wait to beat the purple team in about an hour!" Ralph was captain of the yellow team. Sister Rosemary raised her voice only a second time to end the talking and with it, her palm slammed her desk with more fury than necessary over elation from a twelve-year-old boy.

"And for that, Mr. VelDiccio, you will all remain in this classroom until the sun sets and then some. You will all walk home in the dark. Since you can't keep your pesky mouths shut."

The kickball tournament was ruined, as it rained for the next two days, and they all lost the momentum and energy to find a new day. They had carefully selected that fated Tuesday based on the neighborhood's agreement and the weather forecast. Instead, they all walked home in the dark to very angry parents. Angry for talking. Angry for disrespecting a nun's command. Angry for enthusiasm over a game. We were wrong. Sister was right.

Clem marveled at the necklace in between bubble blows, likely in the middle of some fairytale scenario in her brain. It was the perfect weather for it. Katrina didn't want to crush her with the truth about the beads, so she challenged herself to switch gears. She rested the paint brushes in the trays and threw on her gardening gloves. The cucumber garden bed needed weeding. She bent down and zeroed in on a new memory. Her third-grade teacher who wasn't a nun read them novels that she probably wasn't supposed to: *The Wizard of Oz* by Frank L. Baum. Every day of third grade at precisely 10:15 a.m. made school worth waking up for at 7 a.m. Katrina and her best friend at the time, Willa, couldn't wait for each next chapter. Ms. Denning stretched her words and animated the characters. And any time the head nun would surprise her with an afternoon visit, she'd close the book and shove it into her pants in the back. It was glorious. She and Willa adored Ms. Denning for the rebellion. Even if it was the only thing she did to rebel. If you're going to rebel, a forbidden novel was the way to go. She was a compassionate teacher who told them to create their own happiness when no one else cooperated. She told them that rules were for following, but occasionally it was okay to be inquisitive and explore other ways. None of us knew at the time that the novel wasn't on the curriculum. It wasn't until years later that we figured it out.

"Mama, please tell me what the beads do?" Katrina knew her answer would affect her daughter for years. She had to make the thoughtful choice. The choice that would best serve her child. Katrina glanced at the beads, the fence, the beautiful day, then found the words.

"Clem. The necklace will be what you choose it to be. The goodness you choose for it will be stronger than any words someone else could teach you."

DAPHNE

The abandon of my poisonous shoveling habit requires the adoption of a new one: one with confection, one that won't kill me. The sugar makes my head and intestines throb to the count of eight: "I Got a Crush on You" by the Jets. Upon jamming a handful of bears in my mouth I feel nothing short of elation in the form of gelatinous bears, shiny coats, bendy bliss. Jacked-up senses. I feel it all over my pulse, stretched out like my pre-teen jelly shoes in July of 1985.

We must part, as my insides twist from their gorgeous pangs and citrus bent. Within an hour of shoving a lump of bears in my mouth I plant face down on my bedspread. The pressure, the bristle, they no longer respect my love for them. Damn them for wrestling with my brain science and my intestinal tract.

Pears are my new bears: Mom sent an ungodly amount of Anjou pears. "They're satisfying and sweet, Daphne. Slice them, quarter them, Daphne." I have enough for a small tree in my powder room. "Drizzle honey, Daphne."

My escape will be painted in insomnia for sure. I rinse every Anjou from the splintery crate delivered to my porch by Birch Magic, LLC. Mom's notecard—*Enjoy the pears!* Within moments, I'm weary from the effort of rinsing every Anjou, and now they line my counter while a half-full, five-pound bag of bears giggle, wanting me to fail. You want me to fail?

I slap the bag and shove it up, up, up behind Rice Krispies in the pantry. I ask the bears to let me progress in my new exocarp therapy to the tune of Cyndi—I want to have fun too.

Anjous, shall we? I slice the prettiest thin crescents, from side to side of imperfect fruit angled next to cheddar squares, sharp as Madonna's cheekbones in Spain in 1996. They'd make the perfect salty and sweet lunch for a pop star.

The bears giggle. Why so funny? Maybe just one yellow bear sandwiched between two crescents? Look, we're all friends. "Imagine the slivers as candy, Daphne."

But pear-flavor disappears faster than bears' stretch on my buds. I tried.

Give me the bears, toss the pears, and let a girl live in her sugary-moan-twist of a habit that might kill her to the tune of The Smiths.

GENEVIEVE

None of us knew what went on in that pale mint-green shack on the corner of 8th and Ocean Avenues—equidistant from the Atlantic Ocean and Lake Bean in Sand Grove, USA, our pebble and café town—our town where the most exciting thing to happen was a bucket of unruly crabs getting tipped over by clumsy tourists and then those same tourists screaming for their life over blue claws that were only trying to defend themselves. I'd pick nowhere else in the world.

The mint-green shack had a wooden four-by-four that secured the door, through a rusty lock, tighter than our parents' lips over Santa reality. We all surmised it must've smelled like Christmas inside, a rumor we started, totally based on the paint color. The gingerbread brown scalloped edges that trimmed its facade made them smell truer.

Those were the years that Popsicle juice permanently stained our legs and life drooled out of our eyeballs all day. We watched fishermen, beachgoers, and storeowners emerge at random times, separately, and they were steady and expressionless, but for a pronounced sheen on their cheeks and knowingness in their gaze. They'd slap that four-by-four into the locks swiftly upon exit, and we were too afraid to ask what or why.

Who invited them? What went on in there?

In October of 2012, Sand Grove was pummeled, sifted, and tossed in a bowl of chaos like the most violent cake batter known to man. Hurricane Sandy changed the town forever, both in appearance and chemistry. That green shack stood firmly, only its paint and wood affected. Just a little bit more distressed and just a little bit softer for the wear. Businesses were in shambles. People's spirits forever traumatized. The green shack tore on.

Four years later, at 3 a.m., I bundle up with my brand new four-by-four and a mallet,

now brazen in my forty-forth year on Earth. I park my bike. The moon scrunches its face at me. I break the lock. There's a three-legged chair from a local pizza joint, a dusty bundle of sage, and a notebook labeled "Quiet Sea" in black marker. Pages filled in different penmanship. Inside it smells like beach and church. Eucalyptus, low tide. I secure the door with the new four-by-four and leave the broken lock hanging. I caress the building like one does a well-behaved dog. Our minds love a good ending with a legacy floating above us. Meditation as old as time. I feel both satisfied and disappointed, all in one beat.

FEATHER CONTINUES

Stone University began with a lot of eye-openers. And not like: "Oh, I discovered this great spot under the cherry blossom in front of the library to study in between classes." No. These were more all-about-me discoveries that weren't pretty. First, I realized that I was not confident in my hotness anymore. Nope. Frump jeans, frump tops, and baggy skirts because the saltine and cheese habit extended through the summer of 1995 and showed zero sign of slowing. In fact, I'd say that cold Little Caesar's pizza slid its way into the clutch part of the lineup. Only, instead of saltine afternoons with Kelsey, I'd eat those goddamn slices cold after my shift at Marty's Music Stand on the boardwalk. And then chase it with a large glass of iced tea. So, even though internally I was still Feather Sierra, on the outside I curled up, covered up, and didn't do the hot-girl strut anymore.

Rico, a cigarette-smoking boy from Yardley, PA saw straight through me upon our first introduction as hallway dorm mates.

"Hi, pretty lady. I see you," he sneered. And I'd lean in his doorway observing him like one observes a monologue by Shannen Doherty or someone like her. Kind of embarrassed for her, but also totally obsessed with her. Rico was like no one I knew back home. Likely because similar to Louis Magenta, class pothead, I never went far enough to get to know them.

"You're hot, I know it. Tighten up those tops, though. Curves aren't the enemy. Strut your shit. Even if it jiggles."

Instead of really hearing what Rico was implying, I moped around for all of September, and instead of heading to the dining hall for dinner like it was a social event, I'd grab a quick bowl of Lucky Charms and bring it back to my room to watch old episodes of *90210* on my small tubular TV which sat on top of my generic bookcase. Sue Yang enjoyed this version of me. She was nice. And very scholastic. One night while eating a normal dinner of what they called pasta and sauce, my door made noise. People were knocking. Who the hell would be knocking?

"Feather. I'm Jen. You're in my Journalism 101 with Dr. Baines. This is Lara. Come with us to Kamy's," she said. Jen was thin and exactly as hot as I used to be. "Come on. Like now. With us." She motioned to the hallway and smiled at Sue Yang. Lara was even prettier than Jen in that Bush/Nirvana/Green Day way that all girls wanted in 1996. The very-easy-to-talk-to-at-parties girl who has *been there* and *done that,* but she was still so clean where it counted with teeth whiter than snow.

"I kind of already ate. Or *am* eating," I leaned on the metal doorframe, pulling my shirt over my gut. They must see me hiding inside these rags. Like Rico. How the hell do these people who barely know me know that I'm a hot girl in hiding? Like is it in my makeup? Had to be. My eyelashes spoke many languages fluently. My lipstick was silver. "You know what? I can have tea or something. Give me a sec."

They stepped into our boring room a little further and that's when I realized the walls needed work. My poster of Madonna sitting at a table in Spain was drowned in white cinderblocks. Mental note: *more Pearl Jam on walls.* Sue waved goodbye as I closed the door with the campus hotties in Army jackets, and I knew it. I knew what she was thinking: *Traitor. I see you.* Oh, Sue. I wish it were that simple. I belong nowhere and to no one. It's never going to change, Sue.

For the next day and every day after, I ate with Jen and Lara. Then Jen pledged a sorority, so it was Lara and me. And with Lara and me alone, I had the chance to see her work her natural and uninhibited magic with her thin but curvaceous body. The wrestling team in the dining hall approved, and I wanted that same kind of approval, as ancient and horribly backward as I knew it was. Feminist in my heart. Backwards in my actions. Or maybe not? Madonna did both. Now so would I. But with this realization of Lara's powers came my fierce epiphany that I had to lose at least fifteen pounds. The saltines, American cheese, and late-night Little Caesar's pizza was about to be lit up in flames.

"You know, you have a great body," I said to Lara one day on the way to lunch. I had swapped my frump jeans for some bell-bottom jeans and a tee that felt way too tight. I swapped my cardigan for my Dad's actual Army jacket that I grabbed a weekend ago at home. Essentially, Lara and I were twins, but for her tongue ring. I couldn't. An extra piercing in my upper ear was as far as I could take it. For now, at least.

"Thanks. I work at it. Like really hard. A shitload of crunches every day," she said. I didn't expect her to be so honest. I liked it. I could do that. I was in. "I could show you."

In that moment I loved her, still unsure if we were really friends or just passing the time while Jen pledged her sorority and Lara found out that I was a band geek at heart, and not truly alternative. Or maybe I was lying to myself, and I was like her more than I could ever admit. Minus plunging stainless steel into my tongue. Though I bet the wrestlers jerked off to that. *Come on.*

She did crunches to “Machinehead” by Bush, twice through. It was impressive. I would add this to my daily agenda. I missed being athletic. This is when RJ Grandman from Roselle, New Jersey entered my world. Why does it matter his origin? It matters because people from north of where I come from have more charisma. There's an urban edge to them without being New York City edge. There's a spark to their drive that puts them ahead of things. There was no sand and sun in their eyes to distract them from getting things done. Roselle, NJ is lined with diners, old factory buildings, traffic, and a ton of mom-and-pop businesses like bakeries and jewelers set in brick buildings. RJ didn't know bashful if it hit him in the face.

RJ caught my attention by emailing me a question about our history project. To the girl with the *really pretty* eyes was the subject line. Since no one except rich kids had computers in their dorm rooms, I checked my email in the stuffy, ass-smelling computer lab at least twice a day. Knowing that if Tim had access in the library, he'd email me. He'd tell me he missed my lips and me, and we'd figure out our plans for the weekend when I came home or he drove up to campus.

RJ soon became a good friend after getting past the flirting that didn't graduate but remained a sweet gesture. Not because I didn't want him to admire me or like me, but because we didn't have that chemistry the way you know you do. We all feel the compatibility when we meet a new person with dating potential. And when it's not there for both, one person makes it clear without saying it. So the thing with RJ was that he made me feel safe. Like I had a true friend. He'd pop by my room on his runs and pretend he was flirting, but I knew deep down he needed girlier nails and huge boobs. He told me up front he was a boob man. I am not your girl.

"You look like an athlete at heart. Want to run with me?" He asked, sweaty and jogging in place outside in the parking area near our dorm. The area where cars circled around. "I can tell by your legs, not that I was staring or anything."

"I am. I was. I can be," I said, brushing out my curls and then pulling my leftover hair from the brush and throwing it in the street. A habit my dad hated, but it's not like hair is pollution, was it? "I'll join you tomorrow?"

"Absolutely darling." He said it with a twang, even though he was as Roselle as they come. Being Roselle means that you know if you ask that person which subway you need to hop on from Penn Station in New York City, they'll know because they have a city sensibility. Being from the Jersey Shore makes you fluent in beach, but being from a northern NJ town makes you fluent in public transportation. I was jealous of that all of a sudden. It made me feel naïve and less important, a beach-town girl with no grid in my head about how NJ Transit operated on a daily basis.

"Did you write that paper yet?" I asked him.

"Soon. I have rehearsal in an hour, and then I'll write it." He stretched out his shins using the curb for resistance.

"Rehearsal? Are you in a band or something?"

"HA! No. I'm a tech guy for *Sweeney Todd* this semester."

"Ah, I see." Everyone I met here had something to keep them tied to the thing. To avoid the in between. Tongue rings, theater, cigarettes, and Greek Life.

RJ left me to finish his afternoon run, Kamy's for dinner, then his rehearsal, and I still had nowhere really to be. He ignited a switch that was halfway up in my mind. I couldn't ignore it. I missed competing and performing. But I also couldn't live in that space too long or I'd miss class. So, with the hour I had in between classes, I popped into Rico's room for a breath of stale air. He wasn't alone. Across from Rico, sitting on his always-absent roommate's bed was some guy. Dirty blond hair, a face full of scruff, and a pair of baggy khakis, also smoking.

"Feather, this is Brett; Brett, this is Feather. Okay, enough. You two can't screw because I said no," Rico said, full-on with every ounce of conviction. Rico was more honest than anyone I had ever met. At least about other people. "You're both hot in your own boring ways, but no fucking, you hear me?"

Brett laughed, but more in a grunt fashion. I slapped my hand over my mouth like a child, uncertain of what else to do to avoid snorting.

"Pleasure, Feather" Brett said. He was kind of corny, but he caught my attention. Lately, that was the case all over campus. I didn't miss anyone back home. So many interesting people at every corner here. "I love your eyes," he said.

Oh, okay. You want in my pants. And thinking about it, I couldn't decide if that was gross or urgent that we get right to it. What was wrong with me?

"Hi. How are you? Where are you from?" I asked, so logically and so flat.

"Levittown, PA. By the way, your friend I saw you with earlier: super pretty. I've seen her with the hippies over in Mann," he said. Mann was the dorm a few buildings over where the Deadheads and Phish fans communed. "You guys are sort of twins, huh?"

"I guess," I said. Rico was right. I was kind of hot, but boring.

"I told you guys. Don't even think about sleeping with each other," Rico reiterated. Little did he know: I was a virgin. He'd have a lot to say if he knew. Or maybe nothing at all. I knew nothing about these new creatures in my surroundings.

The headboard on the other side of the wall was banging something fierce, and the three of us ignored it as long as we could until we had to comment. It was Rico to speak first, thank God.

"Jesus Christ, I'd say get a room, but…"

"Sounds like they're both enjoying themselves, though. So that's something," Brett said. He squirmed in his posture. I blushed but took a seat next to Rico on his bed anyway. His guitar was in his lap, so that was a sort of distraction for everyone. He played a chord. The banging got healthier.

Rico strummed louder. The banging stopped. Then we all looked at each other, thinking it was over until the female in the duet yelled, "Jesus Christ, I'm coming!" At which we all gasped and laughed three different kinds of laughs. Rico's was genuinely rambunctious, Brett's uncomfortable, and mine, more of a WHOA.

Rico's dorm phone rang, letting him know that his taco-topped pizza had arrived, and the delivery guy was waiting in the lobby. "Be right back. Stay on your separate sides, or I swear to God," he said as he left in a hurry.

"Why is he so against whatever he's against?" I asked, realizing Rico's candid nature seeped into my skin in this split second. "You know?" I slouched and bent my knees with such awkwardness that it could be taken as sort of cute. I was figuring it out and leaning into it all.

"I don't know. Why do you think he is?" he asked. He was so obviously saying things that he wasn't saying, like *Don't you think it's obvious why? We are attracted to each other.*

Rico returned before I could reply, thank God. Brett hopped off the roommate's bed and said a quick adios to both of us. I glanced at the clock on the wall and realized I would be late too if I didn't leave, so I beat Brett to the doorframe and told them I'd see them later.

"If I find out you drove her to class, Brett, I'll kill you both," Rico said, lighting up a fresh Camel with a smoker's squint. His determination to keep us from screwing was admirable.

"Oh my God, relax. I have to stop and grab money that Jeff owes me down the hall," he said and slithered by me after I turned sideways so as not to block the door.

On his way out of Rico's room, his hands grazed my waist. The waist that was once two sizes smaller. And in that group of seconds, so much changed for me. I didn't want to be a spectator in this sport. I wanted to be like Lara. The "hot girl I've seen walking around campus." Nobody here knew I was senior class president, or "married" to Eddie, or in field shows every Friday instead of at parties. I'd shed ten pounds of saltines and cheese and the other ten from my childhood. Maybe five more for good measure and the wrestling team's stares.

When I got back to my room later that night, I had two voicemails. One from Jen saying that Lara and I were invited to Delta's winter dance and one from Eddie, my ex. He sounded so vulnerable. "Feather. Hi. Just checking in. You know? The city is cold, but it's all good. Hope you're well. Okay...bye." I deleted it after listening to it twice. Then I called Lara so that I'd stop myself from calling Eddie. Because that would require a real commitment of my ears and heart. And I was staying put in my middle zone.

FEATHER'S GOODWILL

If I'm going to be in the middle of nowhere, I might as well feel wanted beyond the average-pretty-Italian-girl wanting inside my nowhere. I needed to wear something hot. Today, I sort through my dirty clothes to get a grip on my laundry situation, and I decide that it's bad and overflowing. As I sniff my underwear to find the least offensive, I can tell Sue Yang officially dislikes me. She's peering at me over her biology textbook and hasn't said a word in days. I betrayed her and what she thought I was. She thought I was studious and predictable. Everything was changing. Brett might as well have said *come and get it.* Lara gave me the map. I'd transform and reinvent. Muscle had memory. I swear I had heard it somewhere. Or read it. I'd become like Lara, but my own wavy-haired version of a hot girl. And people like Rico, Brett, and RJ would notice and comment, and Tim would never let me go. And I'd be dreamt about. They'd jerk off to me.

I find the Isolt goddess card in the pocket of my shorts and tack it to my dorm wall. RJ brought me a sketch of Isolt, insulted at its miniature size in my room. He used pencil and charcoal, and I felt frozen with utter admiration for his noticing. His commitment to making art for me. Like, who does that for a brand-new friend whom you've barely known for a month or two? I hung it and hugged him, feeling so lucky and certain I had found a friend in him that surpassed most of my high-school friendships already. I hadn't heard a peep from Kelsey in months. And I didn't miss her. Stone University was my home.

First round of business: change my makeup and alter my wardrobe a bit. Goodwill visits with Rico and Brett proved fruitful on random Tuesday afternoons after or in between classes. Before today's adventure in Trenton, I fill an entire black garbage bag with my clothes from home—a bag my mother would kill me for, but if this Brunette Ambition Tour would be successful I had to start fresh, which meant old. Rico told me the Goodwill "taxi" left at 4 p.m. sharp from in front of Lester Hall, and we'd stop for Chinese food after shopping. I had cash to spend on dinner, which would get me at least a bowl of wonton.

In addition to pants, a few sundresses, and oversized button-downs, I tossed my pink lipsticks into a garbage bag. Lara only wore silver and coffee brown on her lips. And Rico wasn't kidding about the pick-up time. Brett's old Buick that he called Tessa pulled up right at 3:59 p.m. I was ready and equipped with forty dollars in tips from my very lucky job at Candetto's. I was one waitress in a room of six tables. It was a circus act for four hours every Thursday night, but I walked out with $150 every time. Which meant I could pay my car insurance in two shifts and then have a little leftover for second-hand clothes.

Despite appearances, Brett drove like my dad—slowly and carefully, so it took us about twenty minutes, whereas if my Mom or I was driving, thirteen. He popped in some Radiohead, and we listened from the one functioning speaker. Our destination was a colossal Goodwill Store on the outskirts of Trenton. The streets were dead and dreary, but this store stood like a chapel for college kids. Couches, chairs, old glassware, and racks and rows of neatly folded clothes. I was sad I didn't grab sixty bucks instead, but God knows I would need the rest for gas to go home for the weekend.

It was overwhelming, not knowing where to begin. This pilgrimage was to provide myself with new choices so I could be hot like Lara. Only two pairs of jeans and two shirts remained in my dorm room closet, so I needed a wardrobe. The first thing that caught my interest was a short sweater. It was two dollars, which I couldn't believe—plums, oranges, and a thin stripe of navy with knitted loop patterns that felt like, *Yeah, I'm wearing a sweater, no big deal.* I held it up to my nose—clean. I threw it neatly over my left forearm as Rico trailed off in the direction of Men's and Brett toward the giant display of hats. Yuck, but I suppose those were properly cleaned like my sweater. I grabbed two fitted tees since my gut was a lot less bulgy and a pair of gray polyester pants that looked like they'd hug my butt cheeks the way Lara's jeans hugged her size-two waist. These were a six. I'd never get to a four, but at least I'm down from my soul-sucking ten.

A half hour later we were all ready to try on our finds. Rico took in a ton of retro band tees. I opened the door next to his room. He'd never sneak a look. He was way too self-absorbed at the moment, and his creed wasn't like that. When I opened my room choice, Brett was already in there running his hands through his thick waves reading a piece of paper that was likely a script for an upcoming audition, so I instinctively whispered "sorry." Only to have him grab my arm and put his finger to his lips.

"Come in. It's just hats. Shh. He'll kill me," he said, pointing to the wall where Rico was surely considering a Blondie T-shirt to get coffee stains on once it was his. "Don't be scared. I won't bite you," he said after I gave him Sicilian dagger eyes. Maybe I wanted him to bite me. I had a boyfriend though. But something about this whole thing felt right. Like part of the reinvention initiation process that I couldn't have planned if I'd tried.

I slunk into the room, my second-hand sweater folded over my arm, and in front of me was Brett, a stack of hats, and two wall-sized mirrors. So many things ran through my head. Would Rico hear us and cause a scene? Would some other dimension and world allow Tim to know what was happening and bring him to this spot to catch us? Maybe Brett just wanted to talk, maybe I was a slut after all? But I think you had to have sex to be a slut. Would Brett be my first, after all? Fat chance. Or maybe it's a state of mind after all.

"Come closer," he mouthed and sat down on the bench in the room, ever so gingerly, so as not to make more noise. "How's it going Rico?" He called over to appear as if nothing was going on out of the ordinary in a Goodwill dressing room in Trenton, NJ.

"Eh. I'm slow. Fat and slow," he muttered from next door.

We both bit our lips trying not to laugh. I shoved my face into the shirt I was wearing because I was nervous as hell. Brett's face seemed plastered in a permanent smile.

"No. You're fluffy, not fat," Brett answered in a pet voice.

"Fuck you," Rico said.

Brett mouthed the word "Hi" to me. I stepped closer, totally closed in on his now-green eyes, the color of his corduroy jacket that looked like it could've been purchased here or Macys. He took my hands in his. Smooth, but not too smooth.

"Is this okay?" He asked. His offer of consent turned me on more than I could handle. More than I ever felt before in my body. I nodded. He had a totally bigger presence than anyone I had ever fooled around with. It was wrapped in something more mature and more...dramatic.

I squatted to be at eye level, feeling this wild silver haze of *oh my God I'm cheating, aren't I?* But he stopped me. "No it's okay. Stand still. May I?"

I stood back up and nodded for him to put his hands around my only-just-beginning-to-shrink waist. Then, his right hand touched the top of my thigh. I shuddered and grabbed the doorknob, ultra careful not to make more noise than necessary.

"Rico, any luck?" Brett said, using his extraordinary vocal inflection. Man, he was good at this.

"Still trying, bitch. You?"

"Not bad. I like a few of what I see," Brett answered, then slid his hand on my hips, grazing his fingers a little downward. I let him. He hesitated to make sure I was good with it all. I was lost in my torrential silver swirl of *I'm cheating right now, but I'm in college, so it doesn't count.* Instinctively, I grabbed his shoulders and bent into the whole thing. He twirled those fingers down my underwear, rubbed, trickled, pressed, and I stuffed the sweater over my mouth while I orgasmed.

"Found one. Not bad," he said over to Rico making more noise with a hanger on the wall so that if I squeaked a bit, which I did, Rico wouldn't notice. I sat on his lap.

I grabbed his face in my hands, kissed him slowly, and ran my fingers over his crotch this time. He was rock hard, but time was running out. He shuddered and grunted, but encouraged me to leave anyway, super careful with the doorknob. I found my own dressing room for real. I was unsteady and dizzy, but completely elated. Shit. Shit. Shit.

Rico paid for three new tees, and I bought everything in my arms. I couldn't even bring myself to peel off my jeans to try anything on. Also, out of courtesy to anyone who tried stuff on after me. I paid for it all. Brett bought nothing, claiming none of it looked like him.

The ride home was enveloped in Rico's band back home called Stretch It Out, a sort of combo of Weezer and Green Day, with just a pinch of Beatles, post-1966. Brett flipped his mirror down and looked at me with a wink.

"Flip that mirror back up, dude. She has a boyfriend."

We both accidentally laughed, and Rico shot me a look from his mirror. This was getting to be more fun than I ever imagined.

"Oh fuck you guys," he said. He knew. Rico reminded me of Santos whenever he felt put out by Eddie and me and our baggage. He didn't appreciate his role as mediator, and clearly Rico didn't either. Though this was more a gatekeeper situation.

Santos was very busy the last month of my relationship with Eddie because there was a lot of conflict, and it drove the third wheel a little nutty. We all had decided to go on a horse trail ride after junior prom. Mira Valdez's family owned some farmland about twenty minutes outside of Cedar, so ten of us packed up tents and camped. The next morning, we all hopped on horses with Mira as our guide and rode through the woods. Eddie and his horse lingered behind me. The entire time was about him making comments under his breath about my restlessness.

"It's only a matter of minutes before you split, isn't it? I saw how you looked at Jesse Longo last night. You barely sat down, Feath."

"Eddie. It was a prom. I wanted to dance," I said, looking back stupidly, risking falling off Brandy, my very lovely horse.

"You wanted to dance. Uh huh."

Brett pulled into the Stone parking lot and told us he'd catch us both later after his rehearsal. I smiled at him, then looped my arm in Rico's. I pinched my remaining gut fat and scowled. This was just the beginning of getting my middle out and getting out of the middle. Frumpy class president was officially dead and gone.

LADY WINTER

In the knots of the bark of your favorite oak, baobab, and mahogany trees sits a door to Lady Winter's quarters. Early November stirs her slumber. Her work is required in the woods and elsewhere—communicating, delegating like a supervisor. She has no form, only a scent and a sensation that is strongest at dawn and dusk. And her best friends are the pines. Mostly because they listen. They listen to her instructions and logic. The cardinals are second in line.

Pine Needle of Summer

The pines of summer speak at a slow pace. Steady words, deep vocals. The phrases drift over the trees with elongated energy so that no one moves suddenly or becomes frightened by their midnight whimper. Heat can be draining, but pines are stronger than most. They emit green without a second thought. All the trees share an understanding and a mutual respect with the knowledge of their own strengths and downfalls. The pine's greatest asset is its ability to bring forth love for the very creature that requires a dose. Today, it's the honeybee. Unaware of the child's fear, it only knows that it wants the sweetness of her liquid called lemonade.

It buzzes in circles and lines around the child's curly-haired head as she sips from the striped paper straw.

"Mommy! The bee wants to sting me!" she cries out. "Get it away!"

"Just stay still. It doesn't want to sting you. Put the lemonade down," the mom says.

But the bee remains. It hasn't yet realized that the lemonade's location has changed. The child continues in fear, swatting and sobbing. Her sister encourages the child to join her in the grass. The bee follows the child.

The Pine needle steps in. Her voice is silver and waxy like its cuticle. The bee's buzz is golden and thin. She tells the bee to find those who love her. Flowers. The child does not love her. Move away.

The bee ignores Pine. Pine is persistent. Pine remembers her instructions from Lady Winter.

Bee, we have tincture in common. We share a cure for the congested. My sap. Your honey. We are alike. Go to the flower, not the child. I would not lead you astray.

"I smell sweetness here. Leave me alone, Pine. Carry on with your oaks and poplar."

Oh, bee. The hydrangeas will serve you better than that liquid meant for the child's nourishment.

Back and forth they spoke. The pine attempting to convince the bee where the love was—steering gently, not harshly. The bee refused to stop tormenting the child.

"Stop running. The bee will leave you alone soon enough," the mom urged.

The pine needle resorted to the musical chorus—the finches. She asked them in the tune of jazz, a bee's preferred musical genre. The finches obliged and finally were able to steer the bee toward the hydrangea bush. The finches sang a jazz medley with the nearby ocean and sun. No patterns, just a zillion sharps and flats racing in diamonds and triangles in the air. Chaotic, but in sync with what humans cannot grasp.

This bee and many others like it found their way to the hydrangea bush until the next child held its sweet summer dessert out in the open like a trap.

Pine Needle of Winter

Grouchy Mrs. Welby complains about the doldrums of winter. Day in and day out she wishes she could move to a warmer climate, but then she'd be far from her grandchildren only a drive away.

"My bones ache for warmer weather. This weather is my detriment. The snow is nothing

but a stinking nuisance," mutters Mrs. Welby to the postwoman on her route.

"Try to stay warm, Mrs. Welby. Some nice hot tea and toast, perhaps?"

"Yes, dear. That'll help for a whole ten minutes," she grumbles and makes her way up her driveway. She pauses before turning her doorknob as only a small gust of wind rattled the evergreen next to her front family-room window.

Pine needles speak Italian in the winter. Creating an opera with the ground—connecting and alternating between dialogue and aria. The opera then formulates a perfume from the pine needle oils. And though Mrs. Welby could not hear or smell the opera, she felt the gust of wind indicating that nature was stirring, warming up its vocal chords.

Mrs. Welby puts her teapot on, at the suggestion of the postwoman. Next, she slides her slippers on, feeling haggard and dull. "This weather. My bones ache," she says aloud to her cat named Ginger. *Meow.* Ginger pounces onto the coffee table and nudges Mrs. Welby's photo album with her nose.

Meanwhile the pine needles on the evergreen outside her window continue in its Italian splendor. *Ave. AAAAAAAAAAve,* the walnut tree close by sneers. The cardinal on the fence hesitates. *AAAAAAAAve.* A squirrel scurries in circles.

Mrs. Welby plops honey into her tea and picked up the photo album. *1972. Winter.* A memory of her children on sleds at the old country club. She sips. Smiles. Feeling warmed up, she walks to the window. She pulls the curtain aside and sips once more.

Leonora Welby, allow our oils to sing its emotional support, as if it were being absorbed

through your skin.

And though she could not hear the pine needles sing, this time in English, she feels their melody. Through her toes and up to her lungs. Support. Eternal Love.

She closes the curtain and strokes Ginger's fur. Lady Winter takes extra care with older humans.

"Maybe winter isn't so terrible," she murmurs and removes the sled photo from its plastic sleeve. "You require a frame."

Lady Winter sleeps soundly come March, and she has the pines to thank.

ALESSA

Mom died. Dad wanted a fresh start. Moving is what people do in these situations. I close my eyelids, clutching the slender paint swatch pinched between gnawed-down fingernails of no color.

First square: "gentle emotion." Behind my eyes—I grip the edges of a bar of lavender soap shaped like a piece of pie floating on moon-white waves. I hear a whisper in my ear: *Alessa, ask your question. You know you want to know. Why did Mom die?*

The wedge of soap accelerates, so I dig my nails into the waxy mass. I peek down at my reflection in the warble of white and purple. I see words in the hazy water: Life is this way. It sucks sometimes. You will miss her as much you breathe each day.

I open my eyes to Dad's cell ring: cosmic. It's Uncle Chip asking dad how the ride is from our old home in New York to Ocean Grove, NJ. This is where bakeries and shops dot the streets near an ocean. He told me about marbles in cement and statues of saints behind hydrangeas. He told me about sand between knuckles, ice cream in artists' lofts, everywhere, joy. He told me we find our place and make a fresh start.

I close my eyes again and press my thumb to violet sky's square. Dad's voice fades as I land on a white cloud in the middle of a deep August sunset. I spot a sparrow, and he mouths words to me: *Alessa, ask another question. Break the barrier. Split yourself.*

Will I find love? Nothing happens. I stand on my cloud. I leap.

I watch the mist form words: *Love awaits. but...*

That's weak. You can do better.

"Alessa, are you asleep?" Dad's voice floats to the backseat.

"Almost, Dad."

"We're almost there, sweetheart."

One more square remains. I descend into Grape Devine. I land in a green field, even though these are supposed to be purple options. I run. I touch green blades of grass until I find grape vines in meticulous rows. No one is telling me to ask a question. No one is telling me to break a barrier.

Where am I? Why am I? Why did Mom leave? I taste a grape the size of Saturn: juicy, Sicilian, vital. This is my color.

We arrive at Ocean Grove. "Can we do each wall a different purple?"

"Yes, Alessa."

We hang Mom's picture where the three purples meet. She'd want it all. Swashing and serene.

SANITA

Sanita chose four pinks. Sample-sized containers shaken by a human named Arbor in the paint department lined her bedroom floor. She bought new brushes, grabbed a few free wooden stirrers, and laid out an old bed sheet for spills. Her bedroom wall to the right of her bed begged for accent. White, although making the room seem larger, got depressing after months of living in her own place. Since she was only renting the apartment, Mrs. Rossi gave permission to paint only this wall, leaving the rest Cottontail White. Pink was Sanita's dead mom's favorite. Each pink sample lighter or brighter than the next. To decide, she had to see each sample in the natural light of this Sunday in September. Fuck those square paper swatches. She needed to see the creamy reality of each color spread over the texture of the wall.

Can number one housed Prom like a satin dress barfing ruffles and poofs at every curve. Nothing original, everything bubblegum. Sanita dipped her brush, wiping the excess on the edge of the silver can, careful to achieve smooth. She fashioned a vertical ribbon of pink on the wall, as Prom shoved memories into her sort of smiling face.

1987—Wendy Barner's ranch-style house for her tenth birthday. Bowls of cheese puffs and chocolate circle candies on her kitchen table, streamers across the ceiling, and Freddy Krueger on the TV in the dark bedroom down the hallway. Sanita hated horror movies, so she frequently refilled her snack plate. Wendy had opened her teal Caboodles organizer on the kitchen table after pizza, so Sanita snooped through the trays of lipsticks and half-empty Sea Breeze astringent. All of the girls rummaged through Wendy's nail polishes, so they had something to distract their eyes once Freddy's knives began slashing skin.

"Wendy was a snob," Sanita muttered to herself. She stepped back to examine Prom once more. She never surveyed her guests about the movie choice. No regard for their preferences. She also insisted on controlling the nail colors for each guest. Sanita got stuck with Mustard Magic.

Below the ribbon of Prom, Sanita angled the brush sideways and formed an S with elongated lines. No drips, everything clean.

Can two: Deco. A frosted lipstick veering into iridescent territory. A color that one might choose to accent a sun-kissed face in June. Sanita dunked the brush in Deco after a healthy stir with its wooden stick and painted it next to Prom, leaving a few inches of white space in- between. She grabbed the side of her head, then her hair in a giant chunk, and pulled as one does with a headache.

1998—Sanita was obsessed with the college years of *90210.* Donna in her bleached-blonde bob and brown lipstick. Clare and Steve are dating. Brenda is in London studying theater and Kelly joined a cult. Sanita in real life, in between boyfriends and college majors. Everything feels temporary. Everything feels deserted after Mom died in May. Everything, empty. She scooped ice cream all summer so that her last semester at school wouldn't be riddled with worry about paying her car insurance. In between scooping she saw Dave Matthews and Alanis Morissette in concert.

"1999 was a much better year," Sanita said to her wall. Again, with a sideways brush, Sanita fashioned a P in script, more sophisticated than the S to its left. She jammed her palm against the white wall, as if it became unhinged, snapped, and Sanita retorted with violence. It had become a terrible habit to slam things because when they broke, like mugs, she had to replace them. Her therapist suggested deep breaths over violence.

Can three: Flutter, closer to Aunt Connie's taste. Upbeat and pink lemonade or a nail polish she'd choose. Her Aunt Connie had a beautiful beachfront home, as Aunt Connie was summer herself.

"What a perfect day," Aunt Connie uttered as she screwed the beach umbrella into the sand. Age seventy suited her and inspired Sanita to respect the idea of getting older. Her aunt defied all myths about getting tired and stiff. "We can go down to the water after we set up," she said. Her skin donned wrinkles, but they spoke poetry, and her smile set the rhythm. Sanita adored her. This pink had Aruba and flip-flops written all over it, which was Aunt Connie's essence. When Sanita was ten years old she watched her aunt for hours as she wrapped presents in the backroom of her gift shop, smoothing every corner and edge. She curled the silk ribbon perfectly with a scissor, so that the recipient had no choice but to savor the unopened box. Aunt Connie was one of those people who truly made the world lovelier by being in it.

"It's still not me. Mom, you'd say it's too flamingo-like," Sanita grumbled under her breath and brushed the next letter beside Flutter's sample ribbon: I. Her I was block-like, like an eighth-grade poem. "No offense Aunt Connie," she added as if she were there watching Sanita. "This shouldn't be so HARD, Mom." Her walls were thin, but no matter. Mrs. Rossi knew Sanita was motherless. Why was choosing a paint so hard though? Colors as identity badges? Do they say so much about us, or are they arbitrary?

The last can of pink was Rosemary's Tulip. Reminiscent of fuchsia, Sanita felt hopeful that this one would excel in the light of the sun. Not too bright, hints of red, and definitive enough to break the boring of the white room. She swiped the color inches from Flutter, the same way she did the rest. This ribbon wasn't nearly as perfect and vertical, as Sanita jogged in place and scratched her scalp as if shaking out sand. Today was more cerebral than she had wished. Today was more nostalgic than she planned. A girl just wants to paint.

2010—Sanita was thirty-three years old. Her marriage was on the rocks after three years of faking it. The color of her sweater matched her blush. He's on stage playing guitar because that's where he always was since the day they said "I do." The songs are hot, the air is charged, and the drinks are flowing. Sanita sipped her seltzer and lime and slapped a smile on her face. He never made eye contact with her. It was bad for business, so his eyes met his skinny young fans. Hours later, fourth seltzer and lime, the walls close in. The songs, ice cold. Sanita's head locked into a web of frustration and fever. They got married too young and for the wrong reason. Being tired of dating was not a good reason. Thinking "it was time to settle down" was not a good reason.

Her eyes volleyed back and forth between Prom, the others, and then Rosemary's Tulip. Dozens of times, scanning the pinks with lost hope. She had more luck choosing a color for a manicure.

She completed her word: S-P-I-LL, the LL as a blend. They were a pair.

"Screw it. You all win. Mom never cared for orderly." She rolled up her sleeves and planted a high, messy bun on her head. "You're working together even though I myself freakin' hate group projects."

With the precision of a French chocolatier, Sanita covered her arms in pinks. Wet, dripping, pink, and thorough. Making multiple coats with no sense of direction, she deemed herself a human paint roller. She maneuvered her arms all over her white wall and let the chips fall. However it landed and pressed was how it would dry. However the pinks mixed and intersected would be the way it stayed. For an hour, she soaked her wall with her arms until the sample cans ran dry and a fourth of the wall remained white—"You stay blank. I have a hunch about yellow."

CONCETTA

Like winter to spring in poetic shifts, my shoes are about to change and I'm feeling despair over the switch-up. A rough break of routine for a person who loves being holed up at her desk space, steaming with coffee, cinnamon, and reruns of *Ugly Betty*. An analog clock, a vintage makeup mirror, and melty candles. A rough break from low-pressure winter to plug-it-in spring when things bloom, including your insomnia and pulse. Sweaty chin, anxiety fever.

My black, untied Docs will soon be replaced by Mary Janes that feel like Gearhead, Pin-up, tulips, and May. Spring does nothing to make me feel renewed like "they" offer. #springsucks

I'd rather wander through the dead of winter with the basic promise of renewal simply sealed in whispers. Whispers that spell out pine-needle syllables. Words like icicle and frost crowd my space, and that's how I feel happy.

Ides of March do not inspire the bookish girl. My cockatiel disagrees. He lives in the present and chirps in sync with April's sunrise. I wish backwards for the snow-capped clean. So fresh and clean with a pop of berry poking through. A gorgeous contrast to my black boots.

And it's not that I don't love my Mary Janes as tightly as I love my Doc Martens that cover me in pluck. It's that the movement that feels hard. The movement from winter to spring is clumsy and gives me a headache. Pollen plugged into my sinus sockets, straight to my brain, making me want to vomit, honestly. The movement from prose to poetry, the movement from coffee-house to daffodils, the movement from silence to sunshine. My winter writerness, allergic to this vernal equinox that tastes like carsick. In the form of an unsteadied shoe. You might as well suffocate me and slap me with pollen-filled pillows.

FROM LAILA

Dearest Andre,

On March 6, 2021, I began an exercise in living consciously. It was a very snowy winter, beginning in January. A winter quite curated to my insatiable taste for snow-capped trees and silent evenings when the moon is Queen and the stars, her disciples. As if the winter high priestesses designed it wholly for me. I don't know what any of that truly means, but it sounds delightful, and that world is where I like to peer into when I type text as I am now.

And so, I became accustomed to walking my dog twice a day in the snow, continuing as it melted—we'd head out prior to 8 a.m. and then again around 7 p.m. When the snow began melting, I started finding objects. I'd ignore them at first. Then, by the third or fourth pass-by of the item, I decided it was meant for me to find and to consider. I began stuffing a paper towel in my pocket so that I could pick the items up and put them in my coat pocket. I'd return home, wash the possible COVID-19 off my hands and the object, and seal the item in a plastic bag. By the end of March, I had enough items to write a book.

There was a theme to most of the items. Every object lent itself to the color red, either being the color red, shouting its language in the root chakra dialect, or the BEWARE-in-blood way. Forces we can't see put these things in my path. That's what I'm sticking with. Hush, you skeptic. I bet you're shaking your head, with a beer in hand. Perhaps someone was trying to reach me. Or maybe it's just life. In all its red, passionate fiery mess of a journey.

My first find: red, curly gift ribbon.

Clearly it blew out of a garbage robo-can after Christmas and landed on the grass, burying itself in the snow. When the lawns were in between snowfalls—those public grass areas of houses near the sidewalks—the ribbon poked her curly face through the wetness and waved me over. Until I paid attention and stuffed her in my pocket.

I imagine she was part of the cellophane wrapping of a jam and cheese basket given to Jean from Daphne after years of not speaking. And not over hatred nor betrayal, but simply an argument that neither can recall in any real detail. Likely it was over a clash in what they'd refer to as virtue or values, not loving one another unconditionally like friends are supposed to love after years. A clash that probably involved so much judging and agitation that, clearly, it was a mirror situation rather than a true narrative. Or not. Anyway...

Jean opened her jams, diving for the raspberry first, as her toast beckoned for accompaniment. Her coffee, the perfect temperature this chilly January Sunday, just tickling the first week of the year 2021. With little effort, the delicate jar of *J'Menu* raspberry jam twisted open with a miniature pop! The fruity untouched spread under Jean's nose lengthened her smile. Then, she cringed at the thought of Daphne thinking this basket would fix the fact that she made that horrible decision a decade ago. She should've kept her mouth shut. Then again, shit happens. Sure, therapy began painfully and with intense difficulty, but every year unraveled with more peace and satisfaction, exactly how Cher the Magick at the tarot store said.

Jean stuffed the cellophane and its precisely curled ribbonry into the kitchen garbage that silently closed if you looked at it the right way. Jean never considered reusing those ribbons as one should. That's what junk drawers are designed for. The garbage was topped to the brim even after a strong press down from Jean. She pulled the ties and lugged the bag out of the plastic bin. Red ribbon waving her eyelashes over the hole of the bag, stretching, reaching, desperate to see more of the natural world.

Jean thrusted the minimally heavy garbage bag over her shoulders and into the bin, missing the ribbon's escape into the wind which carried her to the grass. A day later, the red ribbon was covered in thick big flakes of snow, invisible in her winter nest.

Red ribbon held on so tightly for weeks to the cellophane chosen for her. She adorned it with exquisite confidence as adornments do. It's their natural language. Yet, now all she could think about was how free it felt to exist where she didn't belong. Where she was nothing but litter to be recycled eventually or tossed in a land fill somewhere. Shattering the Earth, moment by moment. But right now, she lay in the snow quietly. A fresh start, a little nervous, a little excited.

I found the red ribbon first, and I suppose like birth order, it mattered that she was first. Maybe she was meant to show me that we can let go of our roles given by others? Maybe she was meant to survive the winter because she did, after all, bring some joy to Jean from Daphne in my imagination. Or. Maybe I was supposed to make the Earth a few inches cleaner. Science, spirit, or old Christmas ribbon, I found her, and now I am writing to you about her. Andre, tell me what you think about the red ribbon. How it got there under the snow.

Yours,
Laila

KEENE

Once in second grade Keene threw up all over her desk. Chunks landed in her hair, in Diane Miller's hair, and all over Keene's addition worksheet. It was gross and fishy— mom's tuna salad with scallions. Recess juggled the acids in her stomach and the flow was tipsy. The ball of gassy ick wanted out. They were carrying the one to the tens column. Keene was so humiliated. Her reputation was ruined. The girls on Tendril Place weren't there to help her through that awful year. That was down south in murky Tallahassee, Florida. Thankfully, she moved weeks later. Keene the Puker didn't sit well for her at Sunrise Elementary, kind of like that tuna and scallions.

Even though Keene was heavily mocked by most of the second grade at Sunrise, she recalls Jimmy Bentley feeling bad, comforting her the next morning, saying: "Keene, I think you are fabulous, vomit and all."

He handed her a brand-new No. 2 pencil with a half-chewed eraser and reassured her that she was a superstar. Jimmy was the only bright thing about Tallahassee.

They left Tallahassee a week later when her mom broke up with Jill. Moving sucked. Keene and her mom arrived in Maritime Reef exactly two years after the vomit incident. Tendril Place housed Keene's heart now. It kind of slid right into an open spot on the bookshelf because the girls in the neighborhood were missing spiritual nonfiction. She once envisioned it like that during a koi-pond meditation. Parsley was historical fiction, and Daisy was literary fiction. Keene was the missing piece if they were a bookshelf.

Keene fit in, her vomit incident way behind her. She still searched for that one-to-one bond that was tighter than the rest, and it ended up being Parsley. Did Parsley feel it too? she wondered.

Tomorrow was recycling day on Tendril, so Keene opened the heavy square lid of the blue bin on the side of her house marked Maritime Recycles. With her Mom's heavy-duty kitchen scissors, she snipped away at the large pieces of plastic from gallon milk holders and seltzer-can groupings. Sometimes, Mrs. Calais didn't have time to be as particular about recycling as Keene needed her to be. A few boxes weren't broken and flattened down completely, so she finished that too. A few containers of soup weren't washed properly, so she used the hose on the side of the house. Then, she heard Parsley's groans from down the driveway.

"Hey, Keene. Is your mom around? These onions are for a new jam she wanted to make, and they are extremely heavy," she said, placing the crate at her feet. Their moms were always combining savory and sweet for jams and dips for the business, and this onion variety was no exception. Keene recognized the smell, and in the sun, its odor expanded by probably fifty percent. "Something about an upcoming catering job." Ms. Calais met Ms. DiGrassi their third day in Maritime Reef while browsing the downtown farmers' market. Where else do two vegetable-obsessed people meet? Their business chemistry was instant.

"She's not home now. I'm just snipping sharp plastic and stuff," Keene said. Parsley sat on the pavers next to the garbage pails, leaving the crate of onions to roast in the direct sun. "Drag those in the shade, Pars."

She ignored Keene's request and, instead, braided her hair behind her. "How worried should we be about Daisy? Be honest with me," she asked. "You seemed shaken up the other day after seeing her." Daisy was their favorite friend, and she'd vanished as soon as school let out. Like, she was home in her house, but left Keene and Parsley without a text or a warning. Something was very wrong.

"I don't know much more than you. Which is nothing. Which is why I am concerned." Keene leaned halfway into the canister to grab a few bottles that weren't properly emptied. Mom could be so sloppy when it came to loving her Earth, which was ironic given that her entire vegan catering career depended on that same Earth. She poured the leftover vinegar and water onto the pavers and threw them back into the bin.

"More reason to do something, right?" Parsley asked, completing her braid, wiping her forehead with the palm of her hand, and then finally dragging the onions into the shade.

"No. The opposite. More reason to wait and be supportive like that," Keene said loud and clear. "Seriously, I know doing nothing is hard for you. I get it. But you have to trust me on this. And besides, didn't Daisy kind of give the impression to you that she wanted a time-out?"

She shut the lid of the first recycle bin and moved on to the next that only housed a few items that didn't seem to need her services. A few empty coconut milk cans and more water bottles. Keene really wanted to invest in a good filter for the sink faucet to end this plastic brigade.

"I get it, but then how will she know we care?" Parsley asked. She grabbed a stray twig and tossed it into the street.

"By exactly that. By giving her the space." The air smelled like sour peaches, probably from the actual garbage cans. Keene winced.

"Since you guys are so tight, I will defer to your method," Parsley said and stood to fan herself with her shirt. Then realizing how much space she created between her shirt and her chest, she startled and twisted in disgust. "Yeah…uh…okay."

"We were so tight. Past tense. Now she's a ghost," Keene muttered, holding back a retch from the hot-trash smell.

Keene did not totally understand every nuance of her scientist friend Parsley Lois DiGrassi as she fiddled with the front of her shirt, but continued, "Like I said, I know it's hard for you." Keene picked up the crate of onions and motioned for Parsley to follow her into the house. "It's heavier than either of us should be carrying." Parsley knew how stubborn Keene's streak ran, so she did the invisible spotting thing, knowing Keene wouldn't let go, but at least she'd keep her safe before the enormous crate crushed her toes from a slip of a finger.

"It's just that I think we might want to take risks now. Be bolder about getting her to talk," Parsley said. Once in the kitchen, she removed a couple of stinky onions from the crate and onto Keene's kitchen counter in perfect rows. She knew her mom liked to have those crates returned for future use. Which Keene appreciated because they got reused rather than tossed with the rest of the garbage overflowing her Earth.

"You think I can't be bold?" Keene punched the words out of her mouth. "I'll be bold right now." Something sharp came over Keene, and it overtook her. "Give me an onion." She wiggled her fingers in a *gimme gimme*. This impulse to prove Parsley wrong washed over her.

"An onion?" Parsley asked. "Why? No!" Parsley flicked Keene's extended arm away.

"Yes. Better yet. Peel it, and then give it to me. I'll eat it like an apple." *What in the world am I thinking?* Keene thought to herself. "I need this onion in my mouth."

"Keene. These are the ultra-potent kind my mom finds down in Charterville. You know that. They do well with sweet things only." Parsley's voice cracked.

"I'm serious, Parsley. I'll show you bold." Now she was determined to show her what she could do.

"I am not letting you eat one of these—"

And before Parsley could finish her sentence, Keene pried it out of her hands, peeled the top two layers in record time, and took a bite of stinky, crunchy onion. It took everything in Keene not to vomit before it hit her throat, and Parsley knew that, so she dashed to the pantry for a large paper bag. She ran back to her in time to catch the regurgitated onion after it hit her throat and the flavor registered.

"Parsley…I…"

"I know. I miss her too, Keene." She dampened a paper towel in the sink and handed it to Keene for her pulsing taste buds. "Ugh. That must taste awful."

Rae and Mrs. Calais returned from their errands and dropped a quick hello before heading to the backyard. Parsley and Keene didn't say much more to each other. Keene drank a ton of sparkling water with raw ginger until the onion taste faded. Keene felt it in her bones that Parsley was a good friend for hanging out until the taste was completely gone.

"I'm sorry I was violent, Pars. Your fingers around that onion and all."

"No sweat, Keene. No sweat."

SISTERS WHO BLEED

They bleed like families do: thin, thick, sour, sweet
often at inconvenient moments.

Mauve, as femme as Blanche in her silk robe over coffee or mint juleps—
spits pain out in dots and thin lashes.

It's not unheard of that Osiris's green mitigates the canvas,
the scene, the conflict, but she too can be a sister of rage
if spoken to when she's feeling off-centered or jammed into being a vine or a leaf.

Watercolor therapy for us,
exploitation for them
when they slip into each other's house at the wrong time,

the wrong corner
the wrong pixel
the wrong square
the wrong curve.

Enter indigo's diplomatic charisma, seeking balance, promising light.
Until she's dabbed by the incorrect grey and turns cynical like midnight and damp.
Unable to glow like she's meant, left feeling betrayed over the mix-up.

We see magic and grace, brushed by a skilled hand who knows exactly the
contours, the process of realistic representation.

We don't see what it required of the family—

the patience
the crash
the brush that swept too soon
the finger that had too much caffeine.

Watercolors who run together,
leak, love,
are also eligible for therapy.

FEATHER'S FINALE

It snowed the morning of my last final exam in Comm Law. Dr. Purtnoy urged us to drive home slowly for winter break and instructed, "Keep your radios down. I know you kids." I only followed one of her guidelines and ended up being followed by a cop for probably a mile. He pulled up right behind me in my driveway before I realized his sirens were blaring. I noticed him in the rearview as I crammed my Chevy Corsica into Park. His brow crumpled. I was in deep shit. My dad also happened to be standing at the top of our snowy driveway with his arms folded and a look on his face that read, *I'm gonna kill you, Feather.* I couldn't get my palms to stop being slippery no matter how many times I wiped my jeans. My dining hall Rice Krispies rumbled in my gut. 'Tis the season.

"Young Lady!" The cop began before I could even get out of my car. "I've had my sirens on since Rt. 166 by the 7-Eleven." Yup. About a mile. Shit. Bush's "Machinehead" is a very loud song, what does he want me to do? Gavin's voice masked his siren, and now I'm screwed for sure. I roll up my window, since I love to feel the cold air when I'm driving, wipe my palms once more on my jeans, and open the door to the cop and my dad. The cop belched a raspy laugh that sent chills up my spine. He and my dad were sending non-verbal signals that could only mean I would lose.

"You know what, young lady?" More eerie laughing. "I can see by the look on your father's face that I am not required here. You can take it from here, sir." He walked back into his car after nodding to my dad.

My dad handled it alright. For an hour he was in my face all around the house as I unpacked. He followed me back and forth to the Corsica as I unloaded my laundry basket and swollen tote bags. How I have to shut my "goddamn music and pay attention." How I was lucky he didn't give me a ticket that I couldn't afford to pay. *I know. I got it, Dad.* I didn't say it. That would've landed me a lost set of keys, and I had things to do and money to make this winter break.

We ate dinner as a family in almost total silence, but for my mom's commentary on her most recent hairdresser. "No one in this town can cut short hair right more than once." I wasn't used to this much food at once. I smoothed my gut once over and stopped eating after three forkfuls of linguini.

I sat on my bed after dinner, burping up my mom's tomato sauce with mushrooms. I took out my script for *A View from the Bridge*. I signed up to help out with costumes, but the fussy director insisted we all read it from cover to cover to understand the undertones and time period. By page twenty the house phone rang. It had to be Tim. I stuck an index card from my desk in my script and focused on my tone. "Hello?" I sounded like a very busy employee at Wawa needing the person on the other end to make it quick. Give me their reason for calling during the busiest time of day.

"Hey. What up, beautiful?" He dropped the *s* like I was a friend from his block. Not a good sign. I knew it. I felt the breakup on the brink. Like I was at the edge of Kelsey's pool in October when it's ungodly cold and unswimmable. I hadn't seen Tim yet today, and that was not the way a couple who's super into each other would act. Still, I trembled, fearing that ice-cold plunge into being single. I mean, I always feel single even when I'm not, so how hard will it be? The warmth of a guy's body on me gone. That's how hard. The taste of his salty lips. That's how hard.

"Hey. So I picked up a bunch of shifts if that's cool. I probably won't see you until Sunday." His voice was way too polite. Sunday was three days from now. The next ten minutes of the conversation was like pulling teeth. Yanking on the flesh. Pulpy pain. Blood spill. Edging back toward the middle of nowhere some more. Feather, a fool.

"Maybe we need this space?" he said. Finally, man enough just to say it.

"I guess," I mumbled, choking back a tear.

The truth that he couldn't say was that he needed to be with someone who was all about him: smokes, concerts, and not many things going on in her life. I hung up and instinctively began dialing Eddie's home line. I stopped before the seventh number.

"Fuck!" I slammed the phone and got under my covers with my shoes on. Tim broke up with me because I am not needy. Because I loved my space, soul-wise. Guys at nineteen are so fucking needy.

The next afternoon, totally dehydrated from crying, Santos picked me up. The plan was to find everyone at Drift Mill Pizza at the south end of the boardwalk down in Pebble Heights.

"So, who's everyone?" I asked Santos as we walked from his Nissan across the packed parking lot, then up the boards toward Drift Mill. Drift Mill's slices were the size of three slices of pizza at any standard pizza place.

"Maybe Craig Simms, Meg Barlo, Tom W.," he said, picking up half a clam shell from the boards and tossing it over the dune. He was holding back information, but I had a hunch. We'd basically be having a high-school reunion only after six months of being away. Counting the summer.

"Eddie?" I asked and sped up so I could get a glimpse of the ocean in winter. The ocean was the only view from Drift Mill, separated by boardwalk and an old wire fence. Eddie and I hadn't spoken since senior prom.

"Eh. He wasn't sure," Santos said. He was still holding back. "Maybe."

We walked into a crowded pizza bar and grill and immediately spotted Craig and Meg. I only knew them casually, but they were pleasant enough to be around. "Hey Meg. Craig." We hugged and found a booth next to some baseball players from Cedar North who we'd graduated with. Nods and smiles all around. Pizzas ordered.

Then, I saw him. Eddie walked in with a fresh haircut, shorter than I have ever seen it, and a beautiful girl on his arm. My heart fell into my gut. They were breathtaking. Why were they so breathtaking? Why was I so hot, but so invisible? Because I designed it that way, and then when I feel it, I regret it.

The five of us exchanged quick formalities, like hugs and "Hey, how are you? Nice to meet you." The beautiful girl's name was Lily, and it suited her. She had skin like rose petals and a killer personality. Her eyes were the color of emeralds. I felt my insides scrunch and my spirit fade. I imagined myself floating above the boardwalk in a cotton-candy tornado, but in slow motion. Watching the scene objectively, I saw how much more exquisite Lily was than me. We ate pizza, drank sodas, and talked about our college life. Eddie had met Lily on the track, as she was there watching her brother compete. I could tell she had money, because her makeup was flawless and her earrings, real diamonds. She dragged Eddie to the dance floor, and I felt Santos nudge me with his knee under the booth. I saw with my own eyes that Lily was present. She didn't dwell in the middle of nowhere like I did, complete with a tent and supplies.

"Feath. This is what you wanted, wasn't it? Scrape that puss off your face and come back to Earth." Santos ate two more slices and then signaled that we could leave. We all said polite goodbyes. I only caught Eddie looking at me once, for a brief second until Lily pulled his face her way, like literally. Lily didn't detach from the here and now. She knew what she wanted.

Santos dropped me off and told me to move on. "For the love of God. If you go back him, that will have to be forever." He pulled into the nearest Wawa for a coffee run and left me in the car. I needed that cold air on my face anyway, so I leaned my head out as far as it would reach.

"He'll take you back if you say the words, Feath. But you better mean it." He put the car in reverse and took me home.

"Thanks, Santos. Call me next week."

For the next three weeks I packaged medical supplies with Kelsey at my mom's workplace. We wore hairnets and white lab coats. The work was mindless and they jacked the heat up so damn high that I had a pounding headache by 4 p.m. every day, but it was easy work and I made a couple hundred dollars before I went back to campus at the end of January. Rehearsals and classes started up again. I looked forward to seeing my theatre tribe. I was ready to commit. I'd be with them. Every second.

Everyone on the cast and crew was nice enough, and open to new friends, but they were so loud. Never off. Never on low volume. After every rehearsal, they'd tack on an extra twenty minutes to talk about their performance and why they didn't feel they were "on" enough or how they were too "on." Again, sweet people, but overflowing with themselves and I was starting to get pushed out of this pool where I thought I belonged.

Finally, one night after a strong rehearsal, I up and left. Despite the invite to join everyone in Petra's suite for some tequila and tacos. Their volume and enthusiasm for their lines and characters had gotten on my last nerve.

Instead of being with people, I sprinted out to the campus lake, plopped my bony butt on the bench, and cried myself into the middle once again. I both loathed my new home here and loved it all at once. Every spectrum of Jersey kid smashed together to live in harmony, you'd think I would find the ambiguity comforting. Instead, I still felt in between friends, missing the mark of digging in deep to any one group. Missing the mark of being seen so strongly that I felt that loyalty from them. Maybe I wasn't seeing them strongly enough either? It was all so confusing to my soul, and I didn't know how to fix it.

When I got back to my dorm, I realized I left my wallet in my Corsica because I had worked before rehearsal. I got to my car, unlocked my door, and noticed a box sitting center stage on my hood. Saltines and a shiny goddess Isolt card taped to it...with Eddie's handwriting: *We will always exist in the middle of some other plane. It's just the way it is with you and me. She's the goddess of devoted love. She reminds me of you. I hope you figure it all out.*

It made me sad and, at the same time, hopeful. Going back to Eddie would be the easy way of yanking myself out of the middle. This one I had to do alone.

ACKNOWLEDGEMENTS

To Kev, Mallory, and Lenni—I love you more than all the ice cream. Thank you.

To my dog, the best and sleepiest assistant ever.

For my parents—thank you for everything.

To my active and engaged audience members who pretend to or really enjoy my social media experiments on Instagram. The '80s pop reels. The Bjork-esque romps. The tarot play. Thank you for watching.

Thank you to Jessica Bell who trusts me with words, formats, and extra spaces.

Amie—thank you.

Benita ... we came up with the title together during one of our we-are-going-to-make-our-mark-in-the-world afternoon chats. I value our friendship so much.

Catiie ... you're next. You are.

Corinne ... so much support. So much checking in. Thank you.

To Suzanne ... for your wisdom, friendship, and kick-ass courage. Love ya.

To Malarkey Books for the Feather first pages publication.

To *Cordelia Magazine* for your lovely-ness.

To Ian, Gina, Martha, Kat Collins, Shea, and Kota for your ongoing support and willingness.

Dabinetts … thank you for your unlimited kindness and friendship-via-Battistas.

To coffee—well, you know.

To all of the people who don't feel represented enough in books or life—I will fight and advocate for you every chance I get. I promise.

www.ingramcontent.com/pod-product-compliance
Ingram Content Group UK Ltd.
Pitfield, Milton Keynes, MK11 3LW, UK
UKHW042014190726
13854UKWH00005B/2282

9 783988 320025